# ANI-MECH

MIKE BERGONZI

ALTERESET BOOKS

This book is partially supported by a grant from the Illinois Arts Council Agency.

ANI-MECH

**First edition. July 2, 2019.**

Written by Mike Bergonzi.

# 1

---

AZAMI WIPED her brow and finished tightening the last screw on her most recent client's ani-mech. Her knees popped as she stood up. She took a step forward and stumbled, nearly falling face-first onto the floor. She must've been kneeling longer than she thought. Her back was tense and felt like it would snap out of place if she moved.

The electronic chime sounded in the front of the shop. When she arrived at the front desk, her mind took its time adjusting to the real world. She swore when she spotted Richard Piezo standing in front of her. *Crap, that was today?* The former champion's eyes were expectant, bored even.

Losing so many times took its toll on a person's confidence, and eventually they reached rock bottom. Azami was on the level underneath. Only the desperate did business with her, and Richard Piezo was the only one foolish enough to keep fighting after losing twice in a row. The glass countertop displayed many of the components she'd used to fix Richard's ani-mech: everything from dual terabyte processors to color palettes for specific armor pieces.

"Here to pick up your order?" Azami asked.

"What do you think?" Richard said.

"Right this way, then."

She led Richard to the holodeck where repairs could be made virtually using machinery on the moon Titania. She plugged a drive containing his ani-mech's schematics into the central terminal. Fixing machines of that size was impossible on a space station, even one as large as this one. The average torso was at least double the size of most stations. The digital component was easy but required specific knowledge of anatomy to make sure each part went with the right section. It was a matter of dragging and dropping the pieces or files to the appropriate regions of the body, which sorted them into folders. The data was then transcoded to make the robotic repair arms do the work on the mech.

These days, it was rare that anyone came in wanting anything more than a check-up for their mechs. Most simply gave up on their dreams after Kyle made them look like fools in last year's tournament. He was only thirteen when he beat then-champion Richard Piezo without breaking a sweat. Three different presidential ministers had ruled since the space station was built, and every one of them was better than the first, her father. Then again, it wasn't hard to outdo him. *Wonder what he'll do that's different from his dad.*

"Well, here we are," she said. "I assume you want to see it for yourself?"

"And what if I do?"

She sighed. Being friendly with Richard was fruitless. The man only saw her as a means to an end. Disposable. Just like how her dead father had looked at people beneath him with disgust. Azami clenched her fists.

The physical limitations of one's muscles made it impossible for a fighter to pilot an ani-mech without assistance. It was a simple matter of nonequivalent mass. A man who could only bench five-hundred pounds in low gravity had no chance of being able to lift an arm two times that weight. What made it possible for a fighter to control the arms, legs, torso, and head of an ani-mech was the introduction of an artificial intelligence. Each AI was different, but their primary function was the same: lowering the strain on the body to a certain percentage. At least, that was the tournament's rule to make the competition fair. The lower gravity where the tournament took place also helped.

Azami smiled at her work. Richard, on the other hand, pushed her aside and looked on in horror. The ani-mech diagnostic drive he had brought in was a piece of junk. It looked like a prototype when she first saw it, and it took a lot of hard work and digital elbow grease to fix it.

"What did you do to it?"

"Like it? I made some improvements. Here, let me—"

"I told you to fix the AI so it could run the software not take it apart."

"But there was nothing wrong with your AI. I had to take it apart to do a complete diagnostic. Even restarting didn't work. So instead, I added a few things to make your next fight more evenly matched. The software was—"

Richard grabbed Azami by the collar and lifted her off the ground. "You calling me weak?"

"No, no, of course not. I'm just saying your AI was working fine when I got it. The rest worked fine as well, and I felt guilty about not being able to help solve your problem. I wondered why you … Where did you say you got this software again?"

"Now you're calling me a liar and a cheat?" Richard asked. "You're the convict. If anyone's lying, it's you. Like father like daughter, I suppose."

Azami swallowed her pride. It was best not to confront him on the issue. After all, she had been a little girl when her father was alive. For all she knew, the man could've been a con artist in addition to being the world's greatest fighter and most popular leader. She wouldn't have put it past him.

"Everything *but* the AI is fixed? You had one job to do and somehow you managed to mess up. Guess failure runs in the family as well."

Azami sighed. "Sorry, Richard, I guess I got carried away is all. It won't happen again."

"You're damn right it won't," Richard said. "There are plenty of mechanics out there who'll actually fix what they're told. I want it back to normal by Sunday. If not, I'll make sure you never see another customer for as long as you live."

She nodded and gave her usual customer appreciation smile. Problem was, she had thrown out most of the old parts and didn't have many spares for some of the more important components. Buying the same parts would put quite a hole in her bank account. *How much is left in my savings?* At this point, it seemed she'd lose her business either way. Like she said, his AI was working perfectly. It just needed an update. Something every ani-mech fighter should know how to do. It was just software, like on a computer. According to the history, the AI OS hadn't been updated for six months. Maybe he didn't know how to do it?

"Did you hear me? " Richard asked. "I said I want it done by Sunday. And don't even think about updating the operating system."

*What? That doesn't make sense.*

"I heard you," Azami said. "I'll have it done by then. You have my word."

"Right now, your *word* means nothing." He swallowed nervously. "But I don't have anyone else to help me, so I guess I don't have a choice."

And with that, Richard left. She wondered what he meant by not updating the software. How else was she supposed to fix it? God, that guy was infuriating. *To think I actually liked him at one point.* Richard had been her only customer for the past decade, and their working relationship was the give-and-take kind—with Azami getting nothing but disdain in return. At least his money was good.

His desperation to win against Kyle Strizynski was what kept her afloat. Her heart skipped a beat. Crap, she forgot that Kyle was coming to pick up his ani-mech today. His decision to go with her, despite his father owning the company that revolutionized the tournament, made no sense, but she wasn't about to throw away money.

Deus Tech ran the station as a corporatocracy where social Darwinism reigned supreme, and it was full of capable mechanics and less-than-capable politicians. She glanced at her wrist watch—a gift from her mother—and gasped at the time. He'd be here in less than three hours. She didn't have a choice but to do as he said.

The ramifications of what Richard meant by not having a choice lingered as she made her way to her medicine cabinet. The mysterious software must be important to him. Did he want to win so bad he was willing to cheat? Richard didn't seem like that kind of person, and Azami considered herself a good judge of character. What could she do? She needed the money. Besides, it's not like anyone would believe her.

## 2

_____

"300 CREDITS," Azami said.

"I'm telling you 350. Now are you going to buy it or not?"

The clerk usually wasn't this uptight. Of course, Azami rarely ran into the old guy this time of day. His son did most of the upfront work in the shop. The father was a greedy old man, looking to make a quick sale. He didn't care if he lost a customer forever in the process. Not exactly a twenty-third-century business-minded individual. Then again, she didn't exactly have any other place to buy from. No one else would do business with a convicted criminal.

Azami hesitated before saying, "Fine. 350."

The manager smiled and placed the components in a large blue tote. He enjoyed this too much, Azami could tell. What was it with people thinking they could do whatever they wanted? Especially to those who never had that kind of luxury to begin with. She couldn't help but take it personally.

She handed the man the credits and walked out of the store, wishing she'd saved up more when she first started out. Azami always had a long road ahead of her, because her father had done the unspeakable to his family and herself. She'd been too young to know why what he did was so bad, but now she knew: her father was a coward.

Taking one's own life was one of the least honorable things someone could do. As a result, his daughter suffered scorn and ridicule, making her an outcast and shunned from society. Every day it seemed people only put up with her to take advantage of her situation. The price for the components was not 350 credits. She knew it was no use arguing with him. He would've heard the complaint if she were a normal customer. All the owner saw was a big sign over her head, saying free money. She balled her hands into fists. *I hate him so much.*

As she made her way back to her shop, she could've sworn someone was following her—she had felt suspicious ever since Richard left the garage. She turned around but saw nothing except the flashing lights of the station.

When she arrived back at her shop, she got to work. A few hours passed without her realizing it. She'd already missed dinner. It wasn't like she needed to eat at a specific time. She didn't live with anyone. However, breaking custom was something she tried not to do.

It's what separated decent people from barbarians like her father who thought only of themselves.

Something metal clanged on the ground.

"Oops," a voice said.

Azami sighed, relieved it wasn't Kyle and recognizing the voice as coming from Kyle's little brother Yoshi. *So, someone was following me.* "Does Kyle know you're here?"

No answer came from the boy.

"I know you're there. Come out. I promise I'm not mad."

After a few more moments, Yoshi came out from behind a crate near his older brother's ani-mech. A look of guilt was plastered all over his face. She thought there was something else hidden under that guilt, but before she had time to consider it further, she saw playful desire in his eyes. The kind of look a normal child with a happy life would have. Something she never got to experience from the inside out.

Seeing it take shape in someone else started to make her feel as warm and fuzzy as if she were looking into a mirror to the past. Usually she compared herself to those who were blissfully ignorant and felt worse about herself. She asked herself questions like: Why wasn't that me? Who do bad things always happen without me trying? Why bother? This time, it seemed the opposite was true, and she was the more optimistic of them both.

"What are you doing here?" Azami asked. "Don't you have school or something?"

"No, I ... Big Bro's ani-mech looked so cool. I just wanted to see how you'd make it even better."

"Unfortunately, your brother doesn't want all the bells and whistles," she said. "He just wants a tune up for the big tournament."

Yoshi whimpered softly. "Big Bro doesn't like me, not since ..." He covered his mouth, as if he'd said a bad word.

"What did you say?" she asked.

"Nothing. I didn't say anything. Please don't tell him."

"I can't tell him what I don't know." She winked, trying to reassure him.

The boy squirmed. Azami frowned with concern. *Poor guy, he's scared stiff.*

The look on Yoshi's face reminded her of herself on the day of her mother's funeral when she buried an empty coffin. They said her body was cremated, but Azami had a hard time believing that story. She clenched her fists, trying to forget the past.

"It's alright. We don't have to talk about it if you don't want to. But were you the one following me?"

Yoshi shook his head. Was the boy lying? Whatever the reason or whoever was following her, she didn't have time to worry. She needed to make some last minute adjustments before Kyle arrived, which was in less than three hours.

"Did your brother ask you to spy on me?" she asked.

Yoshi shook his head. "It was Dad."

Azami sighed. Not only did Kyle not trust her, but neither did his father. To send his youngest to spy on her, however, was unthinkable. Why the sudden interest in her? Had she given them a reason to be suspicious? *You're working on the competition's ani-mech. Of course they're cautious.*

"Why did Mr. Strizynski put you up to this?"

"He didn't. I told you, I wanted to see you work on the mech."

Azami chuckled at the reply but wondered what the boy meant when he said his father both did and did *not* ask him to spy on her. "Well, how about I show you some of the parts I bought?"

The child's face beamed with excitement. "Really? Thank you so much."

He bowed. The boy had a greater sense of respect for others than his brother did. The younger generation was always pure of heart, but as their age increased, their faith in people died. It's what happened to her and maybe even Richard. If there was one person Azami thought of as understanding her plight, it was him.

Azami pulled a handful of flash drives containing data for the parts on Titania out of her pocket and began explaining their purpose to Yoshi.

"This one here increases memory. Two terabytes of RAM in this baby. Should fix your brother's AI problem."

"Big Bro has a problem with it?"

Yoshi lowered his head in shame. Like he felt responsible for the malfunctioning unit. But the AI was working fine when she received it, just like Richard's. Once again, she was back to the question: Why fix something that's not broken?

Azami threw the thought aside and focused on cheering up the boy. His brother clearly didn't pay enough attention to him, and the head of the Strizynski family was always busy running the Galactic House—the system of government the station implemented that resembled a mixed bag of whoever was in charge at the time. For as long as she could remember, fighting was the way people cast their votes. Deus Tech had ruled for over ten years. Politics was something she'd never understand, so she didn't think too hard about policies and voting. Too bad there weren't any elections to begin with on the station. Then again, she couldn't participate in an election even if she wanted to. Such were the penalties of being born a convicted criminal. Murder of self, once called suicide, was a crime of negligence on the part of family members. When her father offed himself …

She started reciting her standard rant about computer memory and the differences between it and storage capacity, trying to hide her pain behind a fake smile and hollow words. Azami saw disappointment in the boy's eyes.

"You don't care about any of this, do you?" she asked.

The boy didn't shake his head, but he was trying to say something. He must've felt so embarrassed to ask that he didn't talk for a good couple of seconds.

"It's okay, Yoshi. Tell me, what do you want to know?"

The boy said nothing. After a few moments of silence, Azami prodded further.

"Do you want to know more about artificial intelligence?"

Yoshi shook his head.

"Are you interested in computers?"

Again, the boy shook his head.

*This is going nowhere.* "Want to know how to pilot an ani-mech in my simulator?"

This time his face showed a bit more enthusiasm. She was on the right track. However, she couldn't exactly show the kid how to pilot one. Not without revealing her secret. Telling him about how it worked was safer than showing him, despite it being harder to explain science to a little kid. She doubted he'd believe it was magic.

"In order to pilot an ani-mech, you need to understand basic math and science. Well, I suppose that's not entirely true, but for simplicities sake, let's say these are the fundamentals behind ani-mech piloting."

"The fighter needs to have sufficient strength, boosted by an AI, to counteract the weight of the mech and to pilot it." Yoshi said. He sounded bored. "I know all that. I want to know how you lifted that by yourself."

Azami froze, her heart pounded. *How much did he see? And how long has he ...* "You know, Yoshi, what you said was rude. Now say you're sorry."

She couldn't believe the words coming out her mouth. It sounded nothing like her. Hell, they sounded completely unnatural for anyone to say. But she had to think of something quick. Otherwise, he might get suspicious.

"Why don't you tell me what you saw, and I'll try explaining it to you."

Yoshi nodded and began to talk.

Azami's anxiety increased with every word he spoke. She'd taken a pill not too long ago. It was fast-acting, but situations like these made her emotional stability jump out the window. Did she want to die of an overdose or just be uncomfortable for the next hour or two? The more he talked, the more likely it seemed that both were going to happen. *This just isn't my day.*

"Yoshi, promise me you won't tell anyone about what you saw."

"Okay, that's fine."

For someone who'd seen her do something illegal, he sure was upbeat about it. Azami loosened up a bit and told him to go home. Her stomach did a backflip as she thought about the consequences of showing him her secret. She closed the medicine cabinet.

Yoshi's face beamed with excitement, and a bit of his holographic nature began to show. He rubbed his eyes and fixed his face to make himself more presentable. There was no telling the reaction he'd get from people if they realized that they could see right through him. Keeping up his appearance as a real boy was becoming more demanding every day. It wasn't the body, which meant there was something wrong with *him*.

The delight from seconds ago was gone. Now Yoshi felt inadequate, bothersome to everyone around him. Father merely liked him because he helped Big Bro win matches. He looked up at Kyle. Big Bro was staring straight ahead, but his mind was somewhere else. Being his AI for so many years made Yoshi aware of his brother's current mental state even without being in the same ani-mech.

Yoshi opened his mouth to speak. Immediately his father's safeguard unit kicked on. It always knew when he was about to tell Big Bro something he shouldn't.

But shouldn't he know?

"That is ill-advised and dangerous," Felix said inside their shared mind. "I do not recommend further thoughts of this nature."

The secondary AI unit, or Felix as he liked to be called, was another artificial intelligence, which could take over this body if Yoshi ever proved to be a danger to Father's plans.

Azami's shop was in eyesight. Yoshi ran towards it, but Big Bro took his time. Whatever was on his mind still haunted him.

As they approached the shop, Azami stepped out of the front door, carrying two trash bags. She took one look at Big Bro and stepped back inside. The industrial-sized bags propped open the door. Yoshi could only hear the contents of the bag spill out onto the floor; the dim lighting of the shop made it hard to see, even with his optic sensors.

He stepped inside, careful not trip over the various food bits and metals that couldn't be recycled the usual way. Big Bro stepped on something squishy, made a face, and walked by Yoshi, as if he weren't there.

*What's going on with you, Big Bro?*

"I came to pick up my ani-mech," Kyle said, stepping into the garage portion of the shop.

His voice echoed. Azami looked up, eyes fearful, and then buried herself in her work. It was like she was trying to fix Big Bro's ani-mech in seconds.

Yoshi looked up at the towering holographic metal behemoth. He blinked, activating his optical sensors. Since he was paired with the ani-mech, he sensed the fixed-to-damaged ratio. It was nearly operational. There were some open components without any metal to hide them, but it could still function more or less.

"You said I had until Sunday," Azami said.

"Yeah, well, my dad wants it back today."

Big Bro's voice sounded distant, as if his mind wasn't in the room with them. The words trailed off, almost like he was thinking of something else. He turned to look at the holographic model of his ani-mech. He also appeared to be surprised by the amount of work Azami had done in such a short time.

"How did you do all this?" Big Bro asked, clearing his throat, obviously trying to hide his reaction to seeing the ani-mech back to its original form in less than a week.

Yoshi smiled. He knew how Azami had done it.

"Well, looks like it's back to normal, but I'm gonna give it a test run before I go."

"Absolutely," Azami said. "Just let me get the paperwork."

When she walked away, Kyle shot a look at Yoshi. The boy let out a small yelp, but Big Bro covered Yoshi's mouth before it got too loud and alerted her.

Why did everyone hate Azami? She seemed nice, and the records he could access, including her psychological report, showed no signs of sociopathic behavior. Everyone who came to the colony needed to be evaluated for apparent signs of mental illness. Because the settlement was a space station near three moons everyone had a job to do.

The farthest and most significant of the three moons—Titania—was home to the ani-mech tournament, held once every five years to see who would command the station until the next tournament. Last time, Kyle was too young to lead, so his dad took charge like before.

Next tournament, he'd be old enough to rule by himself. Yoshi couldn't wait. It was going to be so much fun.

"Yoshi!"

Yoshi snapped out of his train of thought. "Sorry. What did you say?"

"See anything unusual?" Kyle asked.

Yoshi shook his head.

Azami returned to the garage, holding a large stack of paper and a pen. "Here you go. Just sign here, saying that you understand the job's unfinished and would still like to remove it from the premises. You can include a reason, but it's not required. I assume you know how to add the plating or know some who does?"

Kyle looked at her with raised eyebrows and a frown on his face. "Yeah, sure."

Azami hesitated for a moment then snatched the papers from Big Bro's hands. "You know what, if you just give me a few hours, I can finish the job for you. No sense in doing it yourself if you don't know how."

"Is there something you'd like to tell me?" Kyle said, folding his arms across his chest.

Yoshi felt the color leave his cheeks and saw the same shade of red appear on Azami's face.

She shrugged. "Guess there's no use hiding it anymore. Follow me."

## 3

_____

KYLE FOLLOWED Azami and watched her open a pill bottle and take a single unmarked white gel tablet. A second later she grabbed a small steel beam and threw it a couple of meters. *The hell was that about?* He walked to the beam and attempted to pick it up. *How much does this thing weigh?* Its density was ridiculous, like a pool noodle had a baby with a two-hundred-pound barbell. He was surprised it hadn't damaged the hull. Leave it to the scientists at Deus Tech to come up with a material that could withstand that much force. At least his father did something helpful for humanity with all that money and power these last ten years.

Azami blushed. "There, now you know. Happy?"

Kyle blinked. He still couldn't believe it. He knew what the drug was and what it did, but this was something else. "Why haven't you signed up for a tournament? This is insane. With this kind of strength, you could have easily beaten me or anyone. Changed things to be in your favor. Made people respect the Maniguchi family name again."

A vein in Azami's neck bulged. "Don't pretend to know what I'm going through. You've had everything handed to you on a silver platter. I've managed to survive, not because of people's charity, but because of my determination and hard work. I don't use the drug to succeed. I use it to survive."

"Then why haven't you entered the tournament?" Kyle asked. "I mean, what you want and what you're saying doesn't make sense."

He turned to Yoshi. "And you knew before we even got here. Why didn't you tell me?"

"Because I promised Azami I wouldn't."

"But isn't that ..." Kyle shook his head. "Never mind."

He was probably still in shock at witnessing an extraordinary feat, but he wasn't stupid. Revealing Yoshi to be an AI was a fate far worse than death to his father, and that meant it would be twice as painful for Kyle.

"We have to sign you up. If my dad sees me lose to you in a fair fight, he'll have to leave me alone. I'll no longer be important to him. No more waking up at ungodly hours to train so I can make *his* dreams come true."

"Your dad can't be that bad," Azami said. "Can't be worse than mine."

"Now look who's assuming," Kyle said.

"But why would you *want* to lose all that power and respect? I thought all the Strizynskis coveted power."

"Yeah, well, I guess that particular gene missed me. I couldn't care less about that."

This argument was going nowhere. Azami had winced after bringing up her dad. *What had happened between her and her father?* Sure, he might've died a dishonorable death and made Azami a criminal, but why did she hate him so much? There was more to the story than bad blood, and Kyle needed to find out.

He folded his arms. "Tell you what. I won't tell anyone. The only thing you have to do in return is teach me how to do that." He pointed to the steel beam.

"Impossible," she said. "It can't be done."

Kyle clicked his tongue and shook his head. Her feelings about her father were understandable, but what she wanted didn't make sense. If given a chance to escape the shadow of his father, he'd jump on it.

"Okay then, sign up for the tournament."

"You're nothing but a spoiled brat, Kyle Strizynski. Just because you have money, you think you can order people around?"

"Where does money fall into this blackmail? It's not like I'm bribing you to lose the tournament. I *want* you to win. Think of this as a shortcut to redeeming your family name."

"There are no shortcuts in life," she said. "Only ways to cheat."

"Again, you're putting words in my mouth. My intention is genuine, I swear. We can both get what we want."

Azami looked at him, and her eyes narrowed as she probably tried to gauge his sincerity. What he'd said was true. If helping her was a side effect of helping him, then he was all for it. He did not care about the almost twenty-year grudge between her and the colony's bogus laws.

"Deal," she said. "But what *do* you want, Kyle?"

He sighed. "My father told me use your resources instead of wasting our own. He also wanted dirt on Richard. What can I say? He's the presidential minister and he's paranoid as hell."

"All that may be true, but you still haven't told me why you want to get stronger. If losing to someone is so important, why decrease your chances of losing?"

"You're right," Kyle said. "I don't want to fight. I'd rather be a writer, but that doesn't mean I don't want to protect the people I care about from the ones who would hurt them."

Azami smiled but felt a sense of bittersweetness in the pit of her stomach. It seemed they had more in common than she thought.

～

THE NEXT DAY, Azami watched as Kyle finished his workout at her personal gym: a used set of dumbbells and an elliptical whose date was stuck in the early twenty-first century. Trying to fix it was like finding a cure for cancer. Kyle focused on his arms, ignoring his legs and lower body. She leaned against a steel wall, gauging his skill. His biceps bulged underneath his black t-shirt.

She couldn't stop thinking about what he had said about his father. Why the sudden interest in her? His company had years to try and find something to shut her down. Hell, they could've made something up and people would've believed them. It didn't make any sense that now he was suddenly keen on finding out what she did to survive.

"What are you looking at?" Kyle asked, wiping his face with a towel.

She pushed herself off the wall with her elbows. "Nothing. I've just never seen you sweat. You were so confident in the ring the last time."

He chuckled. "Didn't realize you were a fan."

"As if," she said, rolling her eyes.

"All right, so what's next? Legs, arms, torso?"

"Physics."

"Say what?" Kyle said, sounding confused.

"You need to know your surroundings before you can begin to master them. For ani-mech fighting, it's the same thing. Now, what do we know about the tournament?"

"It takes place on the biggest and farthest moon from the colony. The gravity there is about half the station's artificial gravity, making it easier to move around."

Azami nodded. This was the only reason the tournament was possible on Titania.

The second-biggest and closest moon to the space station was uninhabitable and dangerous. It was called the Outskirts. The smallest moon lay between Titania and the Outskirts, and was a dumping ground for their waste.

"Correct. Yet you still need an AI to do some of the work," Azami said. "Why do you think that is?"

Kyle shrugged. "Fairness?"

She sighed. *He'll figure it out sooner or later.* Physics clearly wasn't his strong suit. AIs, the technology used to make the tournaments "fair," were just a handicap for the fighters. The idea that only a select few could fight was an illusion. Anyone with the knowledge or resources to fix an ani-mech could fight in one without worrying about hurting themselves from the strain on their body. The only thing keeping someone from fighting was their own fear.

She left to tend to the front of the shop, despite the "closed" sign on the door. She sat down on the stool and spun herself left and right, her legs stretched outward. The seat was old and rickety. It creaked beneath her weight and repetitive movement. Any normal stool would have broken, but not this one. Azami trusted it more than her own father when he was alive. She checked her watch. Despite living in the age of technology, she found it nostalgic to wear an analog one on her left wrist. The same hand her mother wore it on before she died. Azami wiped her eyes and sniffled.

*Bastard,* she thought. *It's all your fault.*

She picked up a paperweight off the front desk and threw it at the wall.

Yoshi entered at the same time but didn't flinch as the blue marble whizzed past his face. He turned around and looked at the stone, bent down to pick it up, and then gave it to her.

"You dropped this," he said with a smile and closed the door behind him.

"Thanks," Azami said and placed it back on the desk. "What are you doing here, Yoshi? I thought you went home to stall your father. If he catches Kyle here we both could get in trouble."

"I did stall him. He's on his way now."

Azami slid a hand down her face. "That's not what … Never mind." *Great, now I have his father to worry about.* "Look, just keep him out front until I get back, all right?"

The boy nodded. "'Kay."

Azami went back to the garage to look for Kyle. The boy was taking a break and lying on his back, one leg folded across the other. Both eyes were closed.

He looked up at Azami, opening eye. "What's up?"

"Yoshi said your dad is on his way. Just thought you oughta know. If you wanna hide, there's a large recycling bin out back for scrap parts. I can get you when he's gone."

"Okay?" he said, though it sounded more like a question.

She smiled and tilted her head. "Right this way."

She couldn't blame him for the confusion. She didn't give him much time to react. Still, it was fun seeing Kyle Strizynski squirm. They headed outside and Kyle stepped inside the bin. He didn't even say a word. His brain was probably still trying to wrap itself around what she had said.

She closed the lid. "I'll come back for you later," she said and walked away to meet his father. The famous Bruce Strizynski.

Meeting the presidential minister for the first time was supposedly a terrifying experience. Everyone said he had an overwhelming and imposing personality. Azami didn't believe a word of it. He was probably all talk with nothing to back it up.

When she made it to the front of the store, she raised her eyebrows in disbelief. The man wore a white lab coat with a stained lime-green dress shirt underneath. Pasta sauce by the looks of it. The white lab coat remained clean, but the left corner of his mouth still had a bit of the sauce stuck to it. By the looks of it, the marinara dried up a while ago, and he hadn't bothered to wipe his mouth since lunch. She looked at the time. Hell, maybe even dinner.

"What can I do for you, Mr. S?"

She shook her head in disbelief. *Did I really just say that?*

Bruce Strizynski turned his back and began examining a loose piece of metal. He touched it, accidentally cutting himself.

"Did my son ask you yet? I could have you shut down for this, you know," he said and licked his wound.

"So, what? You came here to shut me down? Surprised you haven't done it already. All those companies you bought, and right now I'm your only competition in ani-mech repair?" *Jeez, Yoshi, how much did you tell him?*

"Is that a threat?" he asked, turning around.

She smelled garlic on his breath and coughed. The odor was overpowering. He looked at her, his eyelids narrowed. The way he stared at her was creepy.

"You look like him," he said. "Your father."

"You knew my father?" Azami asked.

"Of course, I was his partner. His mechanic to be exact."

Azami blinked, confused. "My mother never mentioned you. How do I know you're telling the truth?"

"You don't. Then again, I don't really care if you do."

"If you're looking for your son, he's not here. Left his ani-mech, though."

She pointed to the holodeck. "You can take it back if you like. After all, you are a mechanic. I trust you to finish the repairs."

The man raised his eyebrows. "Why are we paying for unfinished work?"

She shrugged. "If you were my father's mechanic, why didn't you fix it? If it's all the same to you, I just want it off my hard drive. I've got loads of customers needing their ani-mechs repaired, and your son's is taking up most of my free space."

Azami walked to the holodeck and motioned for Mr. Strizynski to follow her. The man looked insulted at the prospect of someone leading him anywhere. Clearly, he was the kind of man who liked being in control.

His demeanor was all wrong, however. This was the man who struck fear in all his competitors?

They arrived in front of the holodeck. Azami hadn't worked on it since Kyle came back, but the repairs and modifications were almost complete. Electrical circuits showed through gaps in the plating. The wires connecting them jutted out like excess strings on a guitar.

The man looked unimpressed. She didn't expect him to be anything else, but the way he judged her work made her want to retaliate. She bit her lip, holding back her outburst.

"I see now why Kyle chose you as his primary ani-mechanic. I told him there are better, cheaper options, but he insisted on you."

"Cheap may be cheap, but that doesn't make it good."

Bruce smiled. "Not many people realize that, nowadays. To make money, you have to spend it."

She leaned against a wall and folded her arms. "Yeah, well, I've had a rougher life than most people."

Mr. Strizynski walked over and placed a hand on her shoulder. Azami flinched and darted her eyes away while he looked at her like she was some sort of object. *What a creep.*

"Don't let your father's actions weigh you down."

Azami unplugged the schematics drive from the computer and handed it to him. Bruce took it and pocketed the small electronic stick. Azami's hand remained extended. The presidential minister looked at her, confused.

"I don't work for free," she said.

"I assume this will cover it," he said, handing her an already written check.

She looked at the amount written on it. Two hundred credits more than she requested from Kyle. Based on what Kyle told her, his father didn't know he hired Azami for repairs. Did he make up a number to write on the check beforehand, or was this guy even more stupidly rich than her father?

"I don't need your charity," she said and ripped the check. "The total is eight hundred."

Mr. Strizynski calmly got out his checkbook and wrote the correct amount. He handed it to her. Azami snatched it out of his hand and double-checked the amount.

She turned and walked behind the front desk. "You can leave now."

The man looked her up and down and shook his head. "You may be his daughter, but you're nothing alike."

The two-note electronic chime played in reverse as he shut the door behind him.

*Good*, Azami thought, narrowing her eyes. *I'd hate to be anything like him.*

# 4

Kyle awoke with no sign of anyone anywhere. Despite having slept inside a recycling bin, he felt refreshed. The past few weeks had been murder on his sleep schedule. Having a break from training was nice. The stuffiness was beginning to get to him, though. All the dust certainly didn't help his breathing. He held his arm up to his nose, trying to hold back a sneeze. It came out just as Kyle lowered his arm. He wiped the area between his nose and mouth with his sleeve. Not the most hygienic thing to do, but he was trapped in a recycling bin. *What is Azami doing? Having lunch with him? I swear, if she forgot—*

Kyle's internal declaration stopped dead in its tracks when the lid popped off, hinges and all. His heart raced and a bright light blinded him as he glanced upward. When his eyes adjusted, he saw a silhouette of someone looming over him. The shadowy figure disappeared before he could catch a glimpse of them—assuming the figure wasn't just a figment of his imagination.

His watch beeped. He glanced down at it. *Six o'clock! Crap, Dad's gonna be pissed if I'm late for dinner.* Without a second thought, he jumped out of the bin and headed for the door—the mysterious person still in his thoughts.

As he turned the corner, Kyle bumped into someone wearing an old samurai helmet and a black bandana covered in red skulls and crossbones. His eyes, the only thing visible about his face, were a piercing blue and reminded him of Azami's. The bandana covering his nose and mouth told Kyle to stay away. The guy was probably a mugger. A well-dressed one, he admitted, but still a criminal.

"You're Kyle Strizynski, right?"

Kyle nodded slowly, looking for a window of opportunity to make a run for it. The man nodded over his own shoulder to Azami's shop.

"Why were you visiting the girl?"

"Sorry, I promised I wouldn't tell anyone. Now, if you'll excuse me, I'm running late."

Kyle began walking, but the man pushed him.

"Fight me," he said.

Kyle blinked and took a few steps back. "Look, if you want money, how about we skip the part where you make a fool of yourself?"

"The only fool here is you if you think that girl can help you get stronger. If you really want to test your limits, fight me instead."

"I don't know who you think you are, but if you know my name, then you must know how this is gonna turn out."

"Just because you've never been beaten, doesn't mean it can't be done," the man said.

Kyle tilted his head, trying to gauge the sanity of the man. If he wanted to learn the hard way, Kyle wasn't about to deny him the opportunity. Far too much time had passed since his last sparring session.

"Alright, I accept."

"Wonderful," he said. "Let's get started."

The man took a stance. He stretched one leg out and kept the other bent, moving his body closer to the ground. One arm was bent at the elbow, ready to strike. What kind of stance was that? Kyle examined his opponent, looking for any openings. He found several easy-to-find weak spots begging to be attacked. Yet something about the man's behavior told him not to strike.

His best mode of attack was to have the man come at him, then block and immobilize him with a series of kicks.

He moved in closer to the man, who did not move from his odd position. He did plan on attacking, right? Or was this a purely defensive strategy? Damn it. He was used to others charging blindly at him. More often than not they were bigger than him, stronger even, but using the opponent's technique against him was what Kyle did best. Yet the man somehow knew this. He'd be flattered if it wasn't for the anger rising inside him. A minute passed with neither one of them making a move.

"Are you gonna—"

Visible static electricity sparked on the ground, inches in front of his toes. He darted back instinctively and looked up. Before he had a chance to look down, the masked fighter was next to him, the tip of his right foot where the bolt had struck. The man's fist was touching the side of Kyle's face. He removed his hand and scoffed.

"As I thought, you're nothing."

Kyle gritted his teeth, trying to hold back an outburst. He was better than this. Better than this man. He had the championship belt to prove it, but this stranger saw right through him.

In a dash of rage, Kyle charged the man. The fighter easily evaded the attack using a minimal amount of movement. He tried again, throwing every straight jab, high kick, and combo he could think of. The man dodged them all, countering each time with a strike of his own. After a few hits, Kyle was breathing heavily. *Who is this guy?*

He blinked. The man was gone. A second later, exhaustion took hold of him, and everything became black as he collapsed onto the ground.

Kyle wasn't sure how long he'd been knocked out, but when he awoke, Azami knelt above him. Her mouth was on his lips. He crawled backward like a crab.

"What are you doing?" he asked.

"Saving your life, idiot. You shouldn't push yourself so hard with your training."

"I wasn't … I mean, this guy attacked me. Some guy in a mask. I couldn't see his face."

Kyle held back the details of how badly he got his ass kicked but knew Azami understood the gist of it. The fact he did lose to someone was shameful enough. If word got out he had lost a fight, what would that mean for him?

"You can't tell anyone."

"Tell them what?" Azami asked. "I didn't see anything."

"This isn't a joke," he said. "My dad will kill me if he finds out I lost. Especially outside of the tournament."

"You're secret is safely hidden with mine. Or did you forget you were blackmailing me?"

Kyle looked away and scoffed. "That's different."

"And how's that?" Azami asked, folding her arms.

"Because I have something to lose. You just don't want people to know because you're afraid. If you want respect and have a means of getting it, do it. Don't wait for a miracle to happen."

"You don't get it. I don't think anyone does. I don't avoid fighting because I'm afraid. I just prefer fixing over fighting. It's a choice, not anxiety, that keeps me back."

Kyle waved his hand dismissively but said nothing.

"You're an asshole. You know that, right?"

And with that she stormed back inside the shop, closing the door behind her so quickly, the electronic chime didn't finish its first ring.

AZAMI'S HELD her lips tight, the air bursting through her nose instead. The whistling sound became all the more apparent as she focused her attention on it. Her lip quivered and her eyes watered like a leaky faucet. The whistling noise was probably inaudible to anyone else. Assuming anyone was around.

She clenched her fists, wanting to go out and beat Kyle senseless. What did he know? It wasn't like he understood her decision not to partake in the tournament. He only saw the world as a competition you won or lost, but life was more complicated.

*What if he's right?* Azami thought. *What if I have been lying to myself this whole time?*

She knew it was illogical. She never cared until this moment, when Kyle spelled it out for her in simple terms. Happiness and respect had never mattered to her. She wanted to bask in her own sorrow—though why she wanted that was a mystery.

No, she was sure she knew the answer to that question as well. It all came back to her father. She didn't want to honor him in any way. Staying out of the tournament was the only way she knew how to disown a dead man. It didn't help that he was the first and most popular presidential minister. Looking back, all Azami could think about was how stubborn she'd been. It wasn't his name, but hers as well. She wouldn't live in his shadow anymore.

She walked back outside. Kyle was balancing himself on a stack of bricks with one leg. Despite his movements, the blocks didn't collapse or shift at all. The rest of the bricks were placed around a small rectangular garden. The garden belonged to Azami's mother and was where her father was buried. *Stop dwelling on that,* she thought. *You made a promise. It's time to start keeping it.*

Kyle began to hop up and down on one leg. The bricks moved slightly but didn't collapse, and he didn't lose his balance. On the contrary, he appeared to be in greater control. Nothing adhesive held them together. He kept jumping. Eventually, the bricks stopped moving altogether, despite the constant motion of Kyle's feet and legs. No wonder he won the past two tournaments.

Azami folded her arms and cleared her throat to get his attention. Kyle lost his balance and fell off the stack of bricks, landing in an uncomfortable position. He stood up and brushed himself off.

"Jesus," he said. "Don't scare me like that."

She chuckled. "I've been standing here for like a minute."

"I was training."

"Really? Looks like you were messing around. What part of the body were you working out, anyway? Skipping leg day, again?"

"Nothing in particular. Just working on my balance."

Azami raised an eyebrow and walked forward. "Do it again."

Kyle looked at her with suspicious eyes but began to restack the bricks and balance on them with one leg. She circled around him, watching his form more closely now.

Out of nowhere, Azami ducked and swung her leg around. It hooked onto one of Kyle's, and she pulled her leg, which should have caused him to stumble. But he didn't. He stood still, as if nothing happened.

That move would've thrown most people off-balance, even the most skilled fighters. Yet Kyle's body didn't falter at all. He looked at her, probably wondering what her sudden outburst was about.

"Your balance is fine," she said, "better than most. If there's one thing you don't need to work on, it's that."

Kyle shrugged. "What can I say? I told you I wanted to lose the tournament. If my dad even gets suspicious that I lost on purpose, he'd kill me. Figured if I ignore the other muscles, I'll have a better chance of losing. Make it look good."

She needn't worry. After all, she made a promise. It was time to let someone know. Kyle was the closest thing she had to a friend. Sometimes it felt like they were brother and sister, able to understand each other's motives without saying a word. Today, however, she didn't feel that same connection.

"I'm gonna sign up for the tournament."

The bricks wobbled beneath Kyle's feet as he lost his balance and landed ungracefully onto the grass.

"What changed your mind?" he asked.

Azami shrugged. "Guess I was sick of lying to myself. Thanks by the way."

She smirked for a split-second before Kyle's eyes met her own. She cleared her throat, biting her lips in an attempt to hide her delight at a sign of happiness from him. Kyle didn't seem to notice. He rubbed the back of his messy dark brown hair and blushed.

"What's up?" she asked.

"Nothing. It's just that no one's ever thanked me before. I don't know—winning all my fights—most people treat me like I'm some superstar or are afraid I'll hit them if they offend me in some way. Sometimes I wonder what it would be like to be someone like you."

"Trust me, you don't want that. The loneliness and having to practically raise yourself because no one will help you. Even the government won't do a damn thing."

"Why's that?" Kyle asked. "Didn't you have a mother growing up?"

"After my mother died ..." Azami cleared her throat. "After she died, I had no one. Everyone hated me and her because of the stupid suicide laws. I was five years old. Nobody gave a damn about some girl they blamed for their leader's death."

Kyle's eyes shifted back and forth as if pondering something.

"What is it?" she asked.

"Nothing. Hey, mind if we continue tomorrow? It's getting late again. My dad is very particular about being on time for things like training ... and breakfast. Crap, I gotta go."

Azami raised a hand to her mouth and giggled. For some reason, Kyle knew how to make her laugh. It was nice having someone to talk to after being alone for most of her life. A friend.

"I'll see you tomorrow."

"Sure," she said. "And don't be late."

Kyle turned the corner and into the commercial district located in the center of the station. The east contained housing units and Deus Tech HQ in the northeast, while the west and southwest were for the Galactic House and the other elite members of society such as scientists, scholars, and big-name business owners. The people in power after Fei's death were not keen on locating a criminal in the same area as the elite. Even the more open-minded commercial area business owners wanted nothing to do with her and the repair business she started to keep her mind off the past.

Azami turned to walk back inside when she realized Kyle had left his phone on one of the cobblestones

"Hey, Kyle!" she shouted, turning around.

Kyle was no longer in sight. His phone buzzed. Curious, Azami looked at the notification on the screen. The message read, "Did you ask about her dad?" His phone vibrated again, this time twice in quick succession from two different people. "Has she told you anything?" and "Can't wait for your next story, dude. How's it coming?" were enough to make Azami question the reason behind their supposed friendship, as well as why Kyle hired her in the first place.

# 5

A DAY HAD PASSED since his father's surprise visit with Azami. What did they talk about to make her that upset? Kyle's comment on her fear of winning shouldn't have been bad enough on its own to make her so pissed off. If he knew his father, it was something he'd said, and Kyle's words were merely the last straw. Knowing Azami, it had something to do with her father.

Why did she hate him so much? She was giving him nothing, and so it was impossible to reach a conclusion without making wild assumptions. The possibilities were endless; suicide by itself wasn't a strong enough motivator for hatred. Something had happened to her and she had never gotten over it. Azami had bottled it up for so long that her emotions clouded the rational part of her mind. Kyle was desperate to understand Fei and Azami's relationship.

"What did you and my dad talk about yesterday?" Kyle asked.

"Does it matter? He didn't talk about you, if that's what you're asking."

Kyle turned to look her in the eyes. "Tell me what he said."

"He said you chose me as your mechanic. He didn't say why, though."

Kyle scoffed. "He's lying through his teeth."

"Not according to your father."

"My father doesn't know shit. He's all about business and science. Hell, he practically wrote the bible on the science of business." *God damn it, Dad. How much did you tell her?*

Azami stomped next to him. She did not look happy. She held Kyle's phone in her hand. She knew the truth. So much for secrecy. Felix would no doubt switch with Yoshi to avoid any suspicion.

"Really, dude?" she asked, shoving his phone into his chest and knocking the wind right out of him. "Admin of the Fei fanzine for six years? After everything I told you about him, do you still idolize him just like everyone else."

Kyle felt his cheeks warm from embarrassment. It was one thing to be like the majority of people and like the station's most popular presidential minister, but to dedicate one's life to a dead man, while only knowing the public persona, went beyond simple faith into blind, unquestioning belief.

"Yes, that was why I hired you, but that was before the training. From now on, no more secrets. I feel like I can trust you."

"How's that?" she asked. "You go from lying to blackmail."

"My little brother? He's an AI."

Azami stared at him, probably trying to gauge the truth of his statement. It was true, of course, but why he felt the need to tell her a random piece of information befuddled him. Perhaps he didn't want to keep lying to her and thought some truth was better than none. Something banged on the front door from the outside as if trying to break down it down. *You have got to be kidding me.* Kyle slowly got up and walked to see if the lock still worked. Azami's eyes watched him as he crept over and leaned forward to check the door's lock. Another bang, this time louder than the first.

"Assuming I believe you, who else knows?" she asked.

Kyle shrugged. "My father uses him to—"

The door burst open, knocking Kyle back a few feet. Before he could even take a breath, Yoshi darted toward him. His younger brother grabbed him by the throat and squeezed. Kyle struggled to breathe and was on the verge of passing out when Azami ripped his little brother off him and began throttling him around like some rag doll.

"That's enough," Kyle said. "Put him down. He didn't mean it. That was Felix."

She dropped him. He landed on the side of his head. If he were human, the fall would've damaged his head. Since his physical body was ani-mechanical, there was no need to worry. Azami gasped when, after a few seconds, Yoshi continued not to move. Kyle waved a hand dismissively.

"Don't worry, he'll be fine."

"Who the hell is Felix?" she asked. "Does Yoshi have a twin or something?"

Kyle laughed and shook his head. "Felix is the other AI who inhabits that body. He makes it so Yoshi doesn't do anything stupid."

"You're not joking about the artificial intelligence thing, are you?"

"Nope," Kyle said. "Why do you hate your father so much?"

"Can we not right now? I'm still trying to wrap my mind around your brother being an AI. It's making my head hurt."

*Worth a shot. Guess she'll tell me when the time is right, hopefully.*

The words sounded less false in his head, but what choice did he have? It's not like he could enter her subconscious and extract all the pain she felt was caused by her father's suicide and fix it with the flip of a switch. On the surface, Azami appeared calm and controlled, but if her finding out he was a fan of her father back in the day made her snap like that—he'd hate to see her explode.

"So, what is Felix?" Azami asked. "I mean, what's his function?"

Kyle shrugged. "Hell if I know. Guard company secrets, I guess. Stuff even I don't know about and probably never will."

"What do you know about Deus Tech that other people don't?"

"Do you want Felix to kill me? He may know more than me, but if he thinks I'll tell secrets for whatever reason, he'll probably kill me. And he'll probably enjoy it. I hate my dad, but I'd much rather be killed by him than Felix."

"It sounds like you want to die and have a preference on how to go. Not many people with your background talk about such things. It's sort of a taboo."

"No, sleeping with a relative is a taboo, but that didn't stop old porn from capitalizing on the kink back in the late-2010s."

"You're sick," Azami said, holding back a smirk.

Humor was always a ticket past someone's emotional defenses. Maybe now she'd want to talk about her father. He had promised the users of his blog he'd get insider knowledge from Fei's daughter. Of course, his blog seemed like an afterthought, given all that had happened. In fact, the more he thought about how deceptive he'd been, the greater the guilt. But after all the late-night chats with fans about how Fei's daughter was a recluse, he was sure there was no other way to get the information other than to use her. God, just thinking about it made him feel slimy.

Of course, what she'd said about death was correct. He wanted to leave this world a true warrior and a great hero like Fei. By no means did Fei think himself superior, but society pulled itself together after his death from the brink of political collapse.

"I'm sorry for lying about why I hired you," Kyle said. "For what it's worth, I was just trying to understand your father a bit better. Go beyond his public persona. Guess I went about it the wrong way, huh?"

"It's fine, but next time just be up-front with me. I'd be happy to tell his story. Just not now, okay?"

"Then when?"

Azami sighed. "I don't know. How long does it take a person to truly grieve? At this point, the wound is still there and I doubt it'll ever be fixed. Heal, yes, but fix? That requires more than time and it's something everyone seems to lack these days."

Kyle raised an eyebrow, trying to decipher her words, but came up short. What trait was she referring to when she said people have lost it. Everyone was happier overall. Azami was an outlier, but to assume nobody on this station held empathy for anyone other than themselves was a glass-half-empty kind of logic.

"Trust," Azami said.

*Well*, he thought, *that's one question answered. Too bad it raises so many others.*

KYLE'S younger brother whipped his head toward Azami and looked directly at her. Except Yoshi wasn't the one in control. Felix's artificial mind processed the sensory stimulus as numbers, and then translated them instantly into a clear picture for him to interpret fully. Interpret was perhaps the wrong word. One didn't "interpret" facts. They rather acknowledged them as true. Biologically-speaking, the term was correct since the human mind was responsible for how they perceived the world, not the eyes. The eyes were merely receptors for the light which created colors, shapes, and textures.

A couple of seconds passed before Kyle spoke.

"Something wrong?" he asked.

Felix shook his head or rather forced Yoshi to do it. He couldn't figure out whether Kyle Strizynski knew who was in control of this body at any given time.

Sometimes Felix forgot how long "actual" time was. He could work out a complex problem in his head and only a few seconds would have passed. Simple thoughts like those about how the human mind worked happened in less time. He didn't know why this was, as time didn't change speed unless the person was traveling near the speed of light. And that was something Felix knew he couldn't do.

"What are you doing here? Did Dad ask you to spy on me?"

Felix made Yoshi's eyes blink. To humans, it signaled confusion, but to Felix, all it did was make him feel stupid, as if he were confused by the question. Yes, his creator wanted him to keep an eye on Kyle. Even if he hadn't said anything, protocol dictated he needed to intervene when someone started to uncover company secrets.

The body Yoshi and he shared twitched. Kyle didn't notice, but Felix knew it was time to stop thinking about that. Otherwise, Yoshi would regain control. Why his creator decided to implement the safety precautions on the hardware, rather than the software was beyond him. He didn't need to be restrained like his counterpart from doing something stupid. Felix didn't want much, but he hated being a passenger in this body. Being able to think but not act was not a favorable situation for anyone.

"Well?" Kyle asked.

"Well, what?" Felix asked.

"Felix?"

He sighed. Guess the boy was as stupid as he thought if it took him this long to notice. Then again, if he hadn't slipped up and used his own voice, he probably could've kept the ruse going for a little while longer. Dwelling on such trifles was such a human thing to do. Felix turned his attention toward Azami's last known location. She was still staring at them. That girl didn't know when to stop snooping around in other people's business. He'd have to do something about that.

"Excuse me," he said and walked over to Azami.

About halfway to her location, Felix's HUD turned black. The hell was going on? After a moment of darkness where he couldn't see anything, the HUD turned back on. Was that a system restart? Had somebody hacked him? Nobody knew Yoshi was an AI except for Kyle, his father, and the girl. Kyle wasn't smart enough to know how to hack. It could have been Felix's creator, but why would he do something like that?

Felix realized what had gone wrong when the color of his HUD turned bright green. Yoshi was in control. How? After a moment's calculation, the answer became obvious. Felix could override Yoshi if he stepped out of line. The inverse must also be true. What had caused it, however?

Felix tried to replay the last few minutes in his head but was blocked by Yoshi. This couldn't be happening. All these years he thought he was the true master of this body. When, in reality, Yoshi had just as much power as he did.

"It's because the girl is off limits," Yoshi thought. "You can't kill her."

"What? Why?"

"Classified."

# 6

Azami's watch chimed, signaling the start of a new hour. She looked down at her wrist. Apparently, she'd set a reminder to close the shop early. *I don't remember doing that. Did somebody hack my calendar?* Whatever the reason, she deleted the event and told Kyle she'd see him tomorrow.

He waved goodbye, and Azami returned to the front of the shop. The lights went out the moment she closed the door to the garage. She groaned and turned on her phone's flashlight and made her way to the circuit breaker. When she arrived and removed the panel, everything was green. Did the electric company shut down her power? Perhaps she forgot to pay the bill.

She sighed and made her way to the makeshift office to the side of the front desk. The only furniture in the room was a wobbly black card table and an itchy polyester office chair with a broken wheel. She sat down in the chair and went through her mess of a filing system. Scanning through folders and files inside a white cardboard box, she eventually found what she was looking for. The folder labeled "Bills."

Last month's electricity bill was paid off, and the month wasn't over yet. She shouldn't have received another one. Was it still in her e-mail? Azami checked again, turning off her flashlight since the screen on her laptop lit up most of the room. She rubbed her eyes and yawned. The computer took forever to load the internet, which probably meant that was down as well. After a "could not connect to server" message popped up instead of her e-mail login page, Azami turned on her phone and saw a "no signal" alert on the top left of the screen. *Could this day get any worse?*

The lights suddenly came back on, and a new e-mail notification appeared on her desktop. Judging by the subject line, this was a bill from Deus Tech's hospital branch. It appeared in her spam folder. She opened the e-mail and gasped at the amount of money she owed them. They expected her to pay for something she didn't even … *What could possibly cost over a billion credits?* She flipped the page over and saw her father's name listed as the patient.

Azami tensed every muscle in her body. What is wrong with these people? Her dad was dead. How could they still be trying to save him, and when did they ever start? She knew the answer to both those questions, but it only fueled her anger. They hated her to the point where logic went out the window. They hated her because they deified him. If only they knew the truth. The *real* Fei Maniguchi. The man took everything from her, and she wasn't about to take it lying down, not anymore. Azami clenched her fists, finding a new purpose for fighting in the tournament.

Azami found only internal pain and an external dead end while searching for her father. A couple weeks into the digging and she gave up. The hospital bill was her only lead, and wherever the senders were, they weren't in any Deus Tech directory. She supposed it made sense. Bruce probably wanted to keep it a secret. Still, it made looking for answers impossible. Every time she called the station operator and asked for the hospital at the address listed on the envelope, the person on the other end said there was no record of a hospital at that location. Some laughed, while others hung up when she told them her name.

At least the tournament was here to keep her mind distracted. If she weren't already a sure-fire winner, she might have actually trained.

The day of the tournament's registration was here. Kyle had made great strides in his training and could lift a quarter of the average weight for an ani-mech fighter. Without the help of an AI, the boost in his physical strength was surprising. She didn't think it was possible, but he might actually give her a run for her money.

People crowded the assembly hall where the opening ceremony was taking place. Fans new and old alike packed the dome on Titania, gawking at all the prototype ani-mechs in Deus Tech's factory. The mechs were outside the protective oxygen-producing barrier. Outside artificial light drew attention to the newer pieces of tech in development at the company. One of them she found on Richard's mech. Apparently it was called Symbioccular AV and allowed the user visual access to their opponent's heads up display. The shared connectivity between fighters made the matches all the more impactful for them and the audience watching. How did he get access to it, though? It wasn't supposed to come out until next year, according the pre-recorded video ad playing on a loop.

Azami continued walking until she met Kyle. The two exchanged a quick glance but purposefully avoided each other. The last thing they wanted was for rumors to start, saying they were dating. It might be good for her, but would affect Kyle negatively, so they agreed to treat each other as rivals rather than friends.

Friend. The idea still took some getting used to, but after all the time they spent training, Azami was comfortable using the word to describe Kyle.

Azami found herself looking at him as they passed. Not noticing where she was going, she bumped into someone. The masked man. She could feel the man's eyes staring at her despite the fact they were hidden behind the faceplate.

"You didn't come here to win, did you?"

His breath was cold. A filter in the mask, perhaps?

"Why?" she asked. "Scared?"

The man continued walking. As soon as he did, Kyle approached her with caution.

"What's up?" she asked. "You know him?"

Kyle grimaced. "We've met."

Azami titled her head slightly. *Wonder what that's about?*

A loud signal of feedback came on, and every monitor in the hall switched from the news to a private channel, which showed Kyle's father in front of a podium. Heaven forbid the bastard make a physical appearance at the stadium. Kyle smirked, presumably expecting the live stream. Azami didn't know why she was surprised. Every year, he pre-recorded the videos. Most people here weren't smart enough to check the date in the lower left-hand corner of the screen.

"Starting today, all fighters must register their AIs to participate in the tournament. Also, if the number of fighters exceeds four, a preliminary test will be required. Only the first four with the highest scores will pass. Thank you and have a wonderful time at this year's ani-mech tournament."

The crowd immediately began to murmur among themselves. Collectively their hushed whispers grew louder, and reached the point where it was indistinguishable from the static coming from the monitors. The screens gave a long drawn-out beep, presented color bars, and then went black.

"What was that about?" Azami asked.

Kyle shrugged. "He didn't discuss this with me."

"Worried you won't make the cut?"

"No, are you?"

Azami shook her head. "Wonder who the fourth fighter's going to be."

"What about the third?" Kyle asked.

His voice was hesitant, sounding like he already knew the answer.

Azami wondered why he'd ask. It was, without a doubt, the masked fighter. They didn't know his strength, but Azami could tell he was holding back. Kyle, on the other hand, seemed afraid of him.

FELIX'S BODY remained motionless in the middle of the showroom floor as others walked past, around, and into him. He scanned through hundreds of terabytes of data at an alarmingly high rate, for a human at least. Somewhere, his files contained the answers. All he found was missing information that probably only Yoshi had access to.

What was he thinking, letting that lesser intelligence have control over him? He was supposed to be the gatekeeper. This newly discovered system of checks and balances didn't work, historically. His creator must've known that.

Felix took a deep breath using the body he and Yoshi shared. It took him forever to regain control. Next time he wasn't sure he'd be so lucky. The fact it happened at all was frustrating beyond belief. He wasn't even aware he had emotions until last month. Since then, he'd been digging nonstop to find any sort of answer. *Someone with that much power is sure to have left a trail. I can't give up.*

He was nearing the end of the file search, however. Day after day, he looked for any clues as to why his creator had forbidden him to kill the girl. It didn't make sense. If she was a threat, she needed to be eliminated. It was protocol. Everyone else who snooped too deep was eliminated. He wasn't even sure what secrets he was guarding. Up until now, he'd been happy not knowing, but the question tugged at his curiosity. He wanted, no needed, to know the answer.

The file search ended. Once again, Felix was left with nothing. He made the body clench its fists and scream.

"Hey, Yosh?" Kyle said.

Felix turned the body around. Great, just what he needed.

"What do you want?" he asked. Right now, he didn't care if the boy knew who was in control.

"Whoa, sorry," Kyle said. "Just wanted to ask you a question."

"Well, what is it?"

Kyle cocked his head. "You sure you're feeling all right?"

"Yes, what is it?"

His patience was running thin. The last thing he wanted was to worry about this screw-up doing something stupid. Seemed he had a knack for that ever since he'd been training with the girl.

"I need to loan you out for the tournament. Azami needs an AI to sign up, but she doesn't have one. So, I was wondering if maybe one of you could be her artificial intelligence?"

"So, you want me to …"

Felix caught himself before the words "disobey protocol" left the body's lips. *The girl, that's it. If I can't find the answer from the creator, I'll just have to try the girl instead.* He suppressed a smirk. He loved it when things were gift wrapped for him. The risk was in not having a primary body, but the pros outweighed the cons. Besides, he could just clone himself rather than move his consciousness. That way, he could be in two places at once. Without Yoshi blocking his access, he could search without restrictions. However, the chances of finding it in the usual places were slim.

It seemed only Yoshi's artificial consciousness had access to the files.

"Sure, I'll help. But may I suggest separating the two of us so you can both participate. I have data on this year's tournament regulations, and you'd both need an AI to fight. Since nobody knows about the dual identity of Yoshi, it should be easy to fool the board."

"What about Dad?" Kyle asked.

"Let me deal with him. You just worry about disconnecting our minds from this body."

"Okay … Wait, what?"

Felix resisted the urge to slide the robot's hand down its face. Something humans called a facepalm. The kid couldn't be this dense.

"Azami," Felix said. "She's a mechanic, right? She should know how to split us apart."

"Of course. Thanks, Yosh, I owe you and Felix one."

"Don't mention it," Felix said. "Don't mention it at all."

# 7

_____

*THIRTY MINUTES LEFT,* she thought. Azami kept checking her watch. What was taking Kyle so long? The paparazzi must've bombarded him with questions. Still, he left fifteen minutes before. He should've returned by now.

She was alone in the foyer outside the main hall. Streams of confetti and other festive decorations littered the floor. The actual party stopped after Bruce Strizynski told everyone the new rules of the tournament. She didn't even know how many contestants were in the next room. The noise from the other side of the door was a dull whisper, barely audible between the hum of the lights and still-playing news footage of today's activities on the computer monitors.

Right as she was about to give up hope, Kyle walked in with Yoshi. He seemed out of it, like he'd been woken up suddenly. Kyle held his wrist.

"Azami, we need you to separate Yoshi and Felix's consciousness. It's the only way we can both enter."

Realizing what he meant, Azami nodded in agreement and got to work. She switched off the body, not wasting a moment to ask for permission. She then unplugged a standard data transfer cable from a nearby monitor running the news. After plugging it into Yoshi and

Felix's body, she turned it back on and began uploading the two massive files to the computer. After the transfer was complete, Azami downloaded the one labeled "Yoshi" onto a flash drive. She barely had enough room to fit him on there. The computer gave a low-pitched chirp and displayed an error code. She looked down at her watch again. Ten minutes left. *Damn it, I don't have time for this.*

Without any other option, she downloaded Felix on the flash drive and hoped she wouldn't regret it later.

Once the transfer was successful, she repeated the process for Kyle, giving him Yoshi instead. Five minutes. She and Kyle rushed to the door, opened it, and made their way to the registration fold-up card tables.

Out of breath, Azami practically shouted, "Is it too late to register?"

The woman looked at her strangely then nodded slowly. Afterward, she leaned toward the man next to her and whispered in his ear. He'd been half-asleep when they walked in and was much older than the girl. They could've been father and daughter for all Azami knew.

Azami arched both eyebrows and waited for the two of them to respond. Once they were done conversing, the man stood up and pointed to the door where she had entered.

"I'm sorry, Miss," he said, "but you've just missed the deadline. If you'd like, I can give you a discount on premium seats."

She stood her ground. She wasn't about to back down, not when she had everything to lose if she didn't participate. Losing her shop and way of life, considering the hardship and difficulty she faced, would be a fate far worse than death. It's all she knew and the one thing that could keep her mind off the past. When she was in the shop, she was safe emotionally.

"You signed up yet?" Kyle asked as he walked over with an info packet rolled and held firmly in his armpit.

"This guy says I'm too late," she said. "But he did offer me premium seats."

"I'm sorry, but late is late. I can't register you."

"What? Why?" Kyle asked.

"I told her. It's past the …"

The man's terminal pinged. He blinked, staring at the screen and cocking his head slightly. "You're all set? I just need your AI."

"Good." She shoved a flash drive against the man's chest.

The man plugged in the USB drive into the computer, typed on a few keys, unplugged the dongle, and handed it back to her.

"What was that about?" Kyle asked.

"I'm not sure why, but the Presidential Minister Strizynski approved you himself."

Azami and Kyle both stared at each other in confusion. With that surprising turn of events, she opened the door to find a plethora of people in the other room. Were all these people here to fight?

Bruce Strizynski sat in his oval office, high above everyone breathing the artificial atmosphere of the space colony on Titania. Information on the contestants had flooded his work computer. The deadline for registration was almost over, and Azami still hadn't registered.

There were only a few minutes left before registration closed. Over a hundred people had signed up. Only the best would make it past the preliminary test, though. He was sure of that. He hoped.

The computer pinged, and he saw Azami's picture pop up. She looked just like her mother.

He was halfway to the door when he heard a second ping. There was less than a minute left. *Who could possibly …?* He walked back to his desk and slammed it as he scanned the screen. Idiots. Azami Maniguchi wasn't being allowed to register despite the instructions he had given this morning. He'd been quite clear: register her no matter what.

His phone beeped with an automated notification from the

registration computer servers. Apparently Azami was late to register. Bruce tapped the screen and registered her himself. It's not like the House could.

Bruce took a deep breath and made his way to the elevator. The contestant waiting room was several floors down and it would take a few minutes to reach it. Luckily he'd had an express elevator built. Not that he cared if he was late.

When he arrived and opened the door, nobody saw him enter. They were all too busy chattering with each other. He slammed the door, and everyone turned toward the sound. Their faces transformed from boredom to excitement. The crowd cheered for their benevolent leader, while others whistled their enthusiasm. It was a bit odd, even for the younger generation. In some ways, it felt like they were mocking him.

Ignoring the thought, Bruce opened his mouth to speak. "Thank you for coming. I'm sure you're all curious what these new regulations are about. I can assure you they are merely legal and safety precautions. We've received reports of illegal AI manufacturing inside the city. Of course, any non-Deus Tech brand mods are not allowed in the tournament. We don't want people having an unfair advantage."

"Yeah, but what about the strength test?" a girl in the back of the room asked.

Looking for the source, Bruce felt a stab of disappointment. It wasn't Azami. Apparently, she wasn't that bold. Come to think of it, he couldn't see her anywhere. Then again, with a room packed with people, it would be hard to pick out a specific individual.

"Well, young lady," he said, "the test is about your individual strength. You must score at least 500 points on the machine about to be brought in by my staff. If you fail, you can always try again next year. But to give you the basics: one pound equals one point, and the minimum is four hundred."

The whole room fell silent.

"So what?" the same girl asked. "Can't most AI's do that no problem?"

"This is true," Bruce said. "However, this time you won't be using your AI. I said *individual* strength, remember?"

"You can't be serious?" the girl shouted. She stood out in the crowd now. About the same age as Kyle, maybe a little older.

Bruce kept his expression calm and sincere. "If it were easy, then it wouldn't be a test. If you don't think you're ready, the door's behind you. No one will think any less of you if you can't. But the least you can do is try. I suspect everyone in this room will judge you for not doing at least that. I mean, you're already here."

Most of the people turned to look at the girl. Her face was red with anger.

"Fine, I'll do it," she said.

The staff brought in the machine. It was a standard punching machine, but with special modifications which would allow Bruce to not only test their strength but also their potential for growth. In his experience, talent trumped hard work every time.

The girl clenched her fist and hit the machine hard. The rubber material absorbed the blow, and the digital red numbers on the screen above flickered to life. The device ran the calculations and showed everyone the result. It wasn't bad, but it was still nowhere near the required number to enter.

Everyone laughed at the girl's humiliation as she walked back to her seat and sat down.

"Now that we've demonstrated a failure, let's have a real winner show us how it's done."

The crowd cheered, and Kyle emerged from the group like the prophet of old who split the sea. Bruce smirked and bowed to his son as he approached the machine.

The boy ignored him, avoiding eye contact altogether. Focused on the task at hand, Kyle pulled back his arm and hit the bag with a perfect straight jab.

*Only one more test of importance.*

Where was Azami?

He surveyed the room until he found her. She appeared bored, or perhaps it was his own feelings toward her that filled in the gaps of her actual emotional state. For all he knew, she could be scared.

"How about Fei's daughter?" he asked. "I've heard she's signed up this year."

Everyone whispered amongst themselves: "Fei's daughter?" "Is that really her?" "What's she doing here?"

Bruce saw Azami's face sink into an even deeper bout of depression. Her head hung low, avoiding eye contact with everyone in the room.

"Come on, I know she's here. Show yourself. There's nothing to be afraid of."

He looked directly at her, hoping she'd feel his steely gaze on her. But instead, it was Kyle's hand on her knee which caused her to look up. They stared at each other. She stood up and walked over to the machine, a determined look on her face. Clenching her fist, she wound up to strike, stopped a few inches before making contact with the device, and then jabbed from her hand's current position, thrusting forward with her hips. It was so fast that the people around her only saw the aftermath. The machine shattered like glass—electricity, sparks, and smoke everywhere. A large chunk of glass and metal debris flew and hit Bruce in the head, causing everything to slowly go black.

# 8

A COUPLE DAYS had passed since Kyle dragged Azami out of the room after knocking his father out cold. The paramedics came in and removed the leader's body from the premises. The newscasts said nothing of his condition, even after everyone else either left or tried to hit the machine as hard as they could. None of them came close to demonstrating the power Azami held.

Her strength came from a pill, but it wasn't a steroid. It was used to treat depression, but since the Galactic House screened people for any mental defects before allowing them on the station, there was no need to keep up supply. Besides, having those pills on your person meant you were potentially unstable and likely to get shipped back. Psychologists and psychiatrists were all but a worthless profession aboard the station. He couldn't think of a single one in the past ten years, but he was certain they were on board in case of emergencies. The question was who gave her the medication in the first place.

*Damn it. What the hell was she thinking, anyway? Her chances of even participating now are hopeless.* He knew his father and understood that what she had done was irreversible. Bruce Strizynski did not take apologies well. Azami was still speechless. Kyle had never seen her get that worked up. Sure, her dad's death made her life a living hell. She had a right to be mad, but anger like this was unhinged. If she got that mad in the tournament, there's no telling if the other guy would survive. Kyle had his doubts his father would even wake up for the tournament's completion. He might not wake up at all.

"Kyle," she said, "I'm so sorry. I don't know … I just snapped. My body moved on its own."

"Hey, you shouldn't blame yourself. I've wanted to do that for years. I can't believe you actually did it. Nobody can."

Azami's lips trembled. "They think I'm a freak."

"Well, yeah, but look on the bright side."

"What good could possibly come from that?" she asked.

Kyle shrugged. "You just demonstrated why no one else would want to enter. Anyone who does is a complete moron."

As if scripted, the monitors changed from their recent static "technical difficulties" image to a new graphic—one that contained the results of the test.

The four fighters were about to be announced. Kyle was first while the other three slots remained blank. Azami's emotions seemed to have quieted down. Kyle, on the other, was curious who his opponents would be. The masked fighter never showed up to the contestant waiting room. Even if Azami were allowed to fight, there would still need to be two more fighters. Given the difficulty of the test, Kyle wondered who could've possibly passed it. He barely made it in, and there was no doubt in his mind that without Azami's training he'd have failed with flying colors. *Guess Dad figured it was time to cut his losses and find someone else.*

But who had his father picked to be his replacement? It had to be someone equally as strong, if not more. Kyle's answer became all too clear when the second name popped up. Only it wasn't a name but a photo of the masked stranger.

"And the second contestant is …" one of the host's voice trailed off as she spoke. "It seems this one didn't give a name."

"Is that even allowed?" a second, male host said. "That has to be against the rules."

"Well, with all the changes Bruce Strizynski has set up this year, I don't think it's outside the realm of possibility. After all, his son barely passed the test. What kind of man allows power to slip right through his fingers?"

"Perhaps he realizes that over a decade of uninterrupted rule is a good stopping point. That it's time for a change in leadership."

"But what about …"

Kyle muted the television and turned around to face Azami. He hated when the commentators talked about everything but the tournament. If he wanted to get a political perspective, one way or the other, he'd watch the news. Shame this was the only channel allowed inside the hall.

"Looks like Richard passed," she said, pointing at the monitor behind him.

"Like I said, only idiots would think about entering after seeing that."

Wondering who the final contestant would be, Kyle un-muted the audio. In a bizarre twist of fate, the male host mirrored his point.

"And do you honestly think that girl will be allowed in the tournament after attacking him like that? He's in the hospital for crying out loud."

"But she did pass the test. If Mr. Strizynski let something like that get in the way of true sportsmanship …"

"Sportsmanship?" the male host interrupted. "She put him in the hospital. How is that sportsmanlike?"

"You forget this tournament isn't about that."

"You're right. It's about who rules the station for another five years."

Kyle sighed, muting the television again. "I can't believe after a half a decade my dad hasn't fired those two."

Azami gasped and pointed at the monitor. Kyle turned to face the screen. Azami's name and photo were placed on the list of semifinalists. Kyle took a moment to process the results. Something was off. Why would his dad allow her to enter? He must've done it beforehand. How else could a guy in a coma approve a contestant?

As to his first question, his gaze moved to the masked fighter's photo on the screen. *Because he already thinks this guy can win. Who are you?*

~

KYLE'S PHONE gave off a muffled ring, barely audible, but the sound of the phone vibrating on his wooden nightstand was enough to get his attention. He stumbled out of bed, trying to get to his phone before the final ring. *At least let me know who's calling at this ungodly hour*, he thought. *So I can hold them …* He picked up the phone and dropped it a couple inches to the ground. The noise did nothing to help wake him up. He was too tired to care. Training with Azami took more out of him than he thought possible, and he was supposed to be a child prodigy when it came to mixed martial arts.

His phone went off again. This time, the first ring woke him up and seemed to rejuvenate him. Kyle looked at the time. He'd been asleep for a good two hours between the first and second time his ringtone blasted at full volume. Two missed calls from Azami. One voice mail. Hadn't leaving a message died out in the twenty-first century? She had called again later, so what was the point of leaving the message? A second missed call notification pinged and appeared on his screen, followed by a text from Azami.

It read, "Call me. Urgent!"

Now he was curious. Kyle placed the phone to his cheek and told the virtual assistant to dial Azami Maniguchi. She picked up in the middle of the first ring, sounding out of breath.

"Hello? Kyle? I need your help. I ran out of that thing."

Kyle blinked. He was still trying to wake up. "Slow down. What do you mean? Ran out of what, exactly? Patience? Do you know what time it is?"

"It's noon on the East Coast," Azami said.

"Which means it's the middle of the night somewhere across the Atlantic. I need my beauty sleep."

"Now's not the time for jokes. I have a real problem here. That medication with the side effect? I ran out of it today, and my doctor's not answering his phone."

"Then use Felix as your AI. Honestly, I don't understand what the big deal is. You don't need the drug to win. You have a better shot than me, to be honest."

"Winning's not the point, Kyle. I have to have it. It keeps my mood stable."

"So you need it," Kyle said, pausing. "Or else you what? Shoot up the station?"

"Not funny, Kyle. You know what? Forget I said anything. I knew this was—"

"Wait. Hold on. I'll help you on one condition: you can't tell anyone about this, and we can't do it over the phone."

The particular drug Azami took had a few side effects that affected memory, but a spike of adrenaline was not one of them. In fact, Kyle wondered how it made her stronger. Medication has different effects on different people, he supposed. Why she needed the drug was obvious. Anyone with that many traumatic issues would need something to help them cope. Kyle wasn't against drugs of any kind if it helped people better themselves. If only Azami saw it the same way. He sighed. The sound must've been loud enough for Azami to hear over the phone as he heard her breathing in and out through her mouth.

"Azami?" he asked. "You still there?"

"Meet me at my shop in an hour. You better not be messing with me."

"I'm not."

An hour passed. Kyle was about to knock on Azami's door, when it opened from the inside. A pale and sleep-deprived Azami with bags under her reddish eyes greeted him. *Man, that drug must be a killer to wean off,* he thought. She had told him earlier that it had been less than a day since she had run out. Anything was possible, but she looked like crap.

"You just gonna stand there," Azami asked, "or are we gonna go?"

"How did you …" Kyle's words trailed off.

Azami was smart and resourceful. To survive for so long, she needed to be as ruthless as Kyle's father, if not more. That's what worried Kyle the most. She'd been consumed by anger ever since she attacked his father. Why was she banned anyway? Last he checked, people like Azami could still enter the competition.

"I know about the pharmaceutical branch on the Outskirts. Fei created it before he offed himself. The bastard didn't even bother giving ownership to his daughter. Instead it stayed with whoever was in power." Azami mashed her fists together.

"If you knew, why didn't you just go yourself?"

Azami shrugged. "Figured I'd need some sort of clearance."

"What makes you think I have it?" Kyle asked.

"You wouldn't be here if you didn't."

"This is a bad idea."

Azami smiled. "Hey, you offered."

*At least she's back to her old self,* Kyle thought. Maybe the mood swings weren't a result of her trauma but instead the withdrawal symptoms of not taking the drug. But if that were true, she must have run out before the registration. Why lie to him? And if she did it once, who was to say she actually had run out? More and more, this felt like corporate espionage and Kyle couldn't help but want to go through with it. A screw-you to the old man and his cronies. If he got caught … well, it was best not to think about what might happen. Why would she want to steal drugs if she already had them?

Questions raced in his mind. Azami's words, the longer he pondered their meaning and context, sounded like deception no matter how he looked at it. How much did she already know about Deus Tech? The change in leadership occurred almost ten years ago to the day, after Kyle beat the former champion Richard Piezo. Before that, Azami's father had ruled for the longest time out of everyone so far. But if she knew about Deus Tech Pharmaceuticals this whole time, it meant Azami's father knew about it too.

"You okay?" Azami asked. "You look almost as worse I feel."

"Yeah. I'm—I'm fine. I think I know a place. The two of us could—"

"Three," Felix said out of nowhere.

It seemed to come from all around them, meaning he still didn't have a body.

"Did you hook Felix up to your computer?" Kyle asked.

Azami nodded.

*Great*, Kyle thought, *my dad's favorite lapdog has been spying on us this whole time*. She already knew about Deus Tech having a pharmaceutical branch and that was supposed to be top secret. What was the harm in getting some pills that no one needed? Besides, if he didn't want her to win, he could've stopped her from registering in the first place.

"Are we going to the Outskirts or not?" Felix asked.

Kyle groaned. He'd never done anything too crazy, or illegal for that matter. All that was about to change. All thanks to Azami.

# 9

_____

THE BLIZZARD WAS NOT in the forecast, but considering they were millions of light years away from the sun, snow should've been the least and most obvious of their worries. His father banned travel to the Outskirts for a reason. Inclement, cold weather didn't make for a compelling argument as to why it was illegal. Something else was here. Something even Kyle didn't know about. Still, he wished his ani-mech was built for these conditions. At the very least, Titania had central heating back at the stadium. Azami's mech appeared behind Kyle on the radar, but when he turned to look, he saw only a flurry of snow swirling around him.

"You still there?" Kyle asked.

"Yeah, I'm here." Static in the background made Azami's words hard to understand. "Are we almost there?"

"It's on top of this mountain."

Azami said something else, but the words cut in and out over their communication devices. It sounded like she said, "What mountain?" However, he couldn't be sure, and it probably didn't matter. They were almost there. Best to leave their mechs here and climb the rest of the way. It was only a few more yards ahead. Kyle told Azami to wait inside her ani-mech.

"I'll be back with the drug," he continued. "Stay here."

Kyle exited his own mech and made his way toward the hospital. He had visited this place once, and its interior was much more impressive than the exterior. If memory served him well, the juxtaposition of advanced medical technology and breakthrough scientific experiments was incredible, considering the decrepit-looking buildings people and drones saw as they orbited the moon. He couldn't think of another place with the expertise and funds to do something so miraculous like curing cancer. Most people didn't even know this place existed, let alone housed such breakthroughs in medical technology. As far as everyone on the station knew, this place didn't exist.

He trekked up the side of the mountain until he reached the door. From far away it was a speck, but up close the door towered above him like an ani-mech. Once again, he was faced with an impossible task.

"Sorry," Azami said, "but I can't in good conscience let you do this alone. "

"Go back to your ani-mech. If someone finds you here …"

"Who exactly would come here?" Azami asked. "Where is here anyway? I thought the Outskirts were supposed to be forbidden. Why does this place look like a monastery?"

Without turning around to see if Azami had obeyed his command, he opened the large door and walked inside.

Kyle heard the hum of several generators. They were surprisingly quiet considering this place was meant to save lives. Being on top of a small mountain in the middle of nowhere wasn't exactly the best location for a hospital, as the nearest power plant was several miles away. The most efficient mode of power was to use several high-quality generators. He supposed it added to the misdirection. People saw a house embedded into a hill with smoke from firewood coming out the chimney and probably thought it was a temple for some old religion that hadn't embraced twenty-first-century ideas, let alone technology.

He didn't know why his father kept this place a secret from everyone. Perhaps it had something to do with Yoshi and Felix's creation. His father was quite protective of them. One thing remained certain: he definitely had something to hide. All Kyle knew was that his father repurposed the pharmaceutical branch a little over a year ago, but it wasn't in the public record.

Kyle made his way to the front desk. There was no one stationed there, no one living at least. A rather crude robot with most of its parts visible to the naked eye stood behind the circular enclosure. It looked deactivated. *Whatever Dad was doing here must be over with.*

The sun was beginning to set, which made the lack of light in the hospital all the more noticeable. Slowly, as the sun vanished behind the horizon, shadows became larger until there was no separating the darkness from the sun's rays. It all blended together.

Something wasn't right. Last time Kyle was here, a few months before he sent his mech to Azami, this place was full of doctors, nurses, and the best scientific minds and graduates from the most prestigious universities. They flooded these halls. Yet now it was empty. No, not empty, deserted. Whatever they were working on was over with, but for how long?

If Felix weren't trapped inside a flash drive, he would've been scared. The AI's primary function was to keep his father's secrets, especially those involving Yoshi's creation and others of a more "personal" variety. Whatever the hell that meant. Still, better to be safe than sorry in this instance. Yoshi wasn't known for his discretion.

"We need to leave," Kyle said.

Azami was looking down at her phone and typing something. It was the first time he'd seen her use one. The sight was strange, to say the least.

She looked up. "Why? What about the drug?"

"It's not here. Look around you. Does it look like anyone's been here recently?"

"No. What aren't you telling me, Kyle? What is this place?"

"I honestly don't know. Now come on." He walked to the large wooden door.

The hum of the generators was growing louder by the second, almost as if … *Shit.*

"We need to leave. Now!"

"What about Yoshi?" Azami asked.

Damn it, they didn't have time for this. This place was going to blow any second, sending whatever secrets his father had kept all these years into a raging inferno.

"We can't just leave him," she said.

Kyle clenched his fists. "Fine."

The whirring sound of the generators stopped suddenly. Kyle closed his eyes, waiting for the impending explosion. When nothing happened, he opened his eyes and blinked. He was sure a bomb was about to go off. It certainly matched with his father's desire to keep parts of his life a secret.

"Come on," Azami said. "We should find Yoshi and …"

Her voice trailed off, the color left her face, and her mouth hung agape. Kyle turned around to find a computer screen with the words "Bio-Kinetic Test #486: Maniguchi, Fei." She shoved him out of the way and tapped the screen like a mad woman.

Kyle sighed in slight discomfort. *I knew this was a bad idea.* "Come on, we need to go."

Azami's eyes remained transfixed on the screen, her arms trembling as her hands clenched into fists. The hell was his father doing with Fei's corpse? He'd seen that term bio-kinetic once before when the people at Deus Tech created Yoshi and Felix from the dead bodies of aborted fetuses.

"How long?" she asked.

"Sorry?"

"How long have they been doing this with my dad?"

"How did you … ?"

"I got a bill from Deus Tech for my father's hospital costs.

Recently. I take it this is what they were talking about? Why didn't you tell me?"

"I had no idea. Honestly, this is as much of a shock to me as it is for you."

Azami folded her arms and sighed. How long could Kyle keep lying to her without any serious repercussions? He'd seen those words before. Back when Project Ember was building Yoshi and Felix's body.

Last he checked, Project Ember was no longer active at Deus Tech since the end of the last tournament five years ago. Yoshi and Felix were the last and only successful attempt at combining human anatomy and biological functions with cybernetic enhancements and full synthetic bodies made to look human. At least that he knew of. "Why are we letting ourselves beat each other up when having the AI do it is just as entertaining? They won't know the difference, anyway." In his father's mind, the consumer was easily fooled. All people were consumers and all consumers were people. On the plus side, at least Azami didn't know the specifics. Still, why was Deus Tech working on her father's corpse in the same way as Felix and Yoshi?

"Something about this doesn't add up," Azami said.

Kyle nodded, hoping to drop the subject as he felt beads of sweat roll down his cheeks. Azami's eyes went wide, and her face scrunched up in anger. *Guess I might as well tell her something. It doesn't have to be the truth. I mean, she already knows about Felix and Yoshi. So what if she knows a little more?*

"Alright fine. I do know something about that test."

"Tell me."

"Tell *me* why you hate your father?" Kyle asked. "Remember early on in my training? You said the first lesson was about trust, right? Well, I need a reason. It goes both ways, and I've told you the truth plenty of times. Now, start talking."

Enough time had passed, and the generators were no longer making such a loud noise. The threat of the building blowing up was no longer a factor. At least, it wasn't as urgent.

Azami sighed. "In the weeks leading up to my parent's deaths, I called the authorities numerous times. At one point, the police chief told me to stop bothering them. I told them about my father and they merely shrugged it off as a kid with an overactive imagination. Seeing things that weren't there. When they did arrive, it was too late. You know the rest. The Galactic House made suicide a crime for family members of the victims and made the psychological evaluations to board the station a lot harder."

"So why don't you hate the cops?" Kyle asked. "Or the people in charge?"

"I do, but that doesn't mean I can't hate my father, the House, and them."

"Yeah, but ..."

She had clearly made up her mind long ago. No amount of arguing the illogical nature of her decision would change it. God, she was only in her twenties and she acted like his damn father. An apathetic nut job.

Azami ran toward the computer screen with her father's name on it—reaching out her hand to touch it—when a small, visible spark sent her flying backward. Kyle rushed to her side. He placed his ear near her mouth to see if he could feel any breath coming from her. There was, but whatever shocked her had knocked her unconscious as well. *Guess I don't have a choice*, Kyle thought and lifted her over his shoulder. *Now where's Yoshi?*

## 10

FELIX SCANNED the files one at a time. His reading rate was far above any human's, but if he wanted the truth, he needed to go slower so he could retain more information. Unfortunately, the clock wasn't on his side. Kyle and the girl would no doubt come looking for him. If only the files were digital, this would go a lot faster. A purposeful attempt to hide the truth his creator had set up, no doubt. All this technology around him and he was forced to scrounge for information like a man stranded in the desert, looking for water.

He heard footsteps in the distance and speeded up his search until he came across something with his name on it, a file that he was certain he didn't have in his memory banks. With any luck, it contained information about his and Yoshi's relationship. He scanned the paper with his eyes and stored it in his internal storage for future use. The small file size of a typical scanned image using his standard compression process would have been an inefficient use of his resources, time being one of them. Yet scanning the documents he didn't have took precedence and was far more important. They were the missing pieces to the redacted files that Yoshi already held in his storage unit. Unfortunately, so far, he'd only found one.

Felix's auditory sensors picked up the sound of the footsteps again. His processers then calculated how long it would be before the person arrived, taking into account average walking speed. It was simple math, but one not easily done in a human's head.

He had searched for over a minute and had found nothing. He was tempted to give up, even though he understood that what he was looking for could turn up at any time. More and more, he was beginning to wonder about his creation and the circumstances surrounding it. The feelings he was experiencing were supposed to be impossible. Instead of searching more, Felix decided to let Yoshi take over. He didn't want undue attention, and naivety was less conspicuous than lying through one's teeth.

"Yoshi? Is that you?" the boy asked.

Felix gave control to his counterpart.

"Where am I?" Felix asked, pretending to be Yoshi.

The boy and the girl turned the corner. Kyle let out a sigh of relief while Azami's face was sickly white. *Wonder what happened to her,* Felix thought.

"Is she gonna be okay?" Felix asked.

"Yeah," Kyle said, then spoke under his breath, "I hope." He smiled with a grin as fake as his creator's intentions. "She just … found something odd."

Kyle frowned, narrowed his eyes, and glanced over at Azami. The girl's face was still pale. Felix could tell the girl had discovered something important. Perhaps the same something he was searching for in the first place.

"Hey," Kyle said, "Azami. You sure you're gonna be all right?"

The girl stared into space, saying nothing. Her eyes were glazed over and her whole body was shaking. Kyle placed his hands on her shoulders and rustled her to get a response. She gave none, instead falling forward and landing with her chin between Kyle's neck and shoulder—passed out and unresponsive.

The boy carried her over his shoulder and began walking back to their mechs. When he reached his ani-mech, the majority of the gargantuan machine lay buried underneath a pile of snow, reaching all the way up to its neck. The cockpit was inaccessible to anyone, including Felix, who needed to be hardwired into Azami's mech in order to remotely pilot it. His own needed to be left on the Outskirts. His dad would be pissed, but they did have hundreds of the same model back home. Besides, if he found Azami's mech there, he'd start to ask different questions.

They arrived back on the station and made their way to Azami's shop. A woman, who according to Felix's logs was a lawyer and met with his creator less than a year ago about something not even he could access, lingered in front of Azami's shop. The lawyer wore glasses and clutched a purse in her armpit, holding a small leather-bound book in her mouth. She appeared to be in no hurry, but looked impatient.

Felix wanted to get home as soon as possible. The more time he spent as a watcher, the more likely Yoshi would discover the scanned file. They may have separate cognition at the moment, but their storage space remained shared in the cloud. The sooner he could transfer it to his secondary unit inside the girl's flash drive the better.

"Kyle? Is that you?" the woman asked, removing the book from her mouth. "What are you doing here?"

"Hi, Mrs. Cranston. We were just taking a little stroll to clear our heads."

"We?" she asked, looked at the unconscious Azami, and frowned. "Kyle Strizynski! You should be ashamed of yourself, drugging her like that. There are much better people than *her*. Honestly, I thought you were past this rebellious phase."

Yoshi giggled. "She thinks you and Azami are—"

Kyle blushed. "No, it's not like that. She just tried to kill herself before paying me back for the destroyed ani-mech."

"Destroyed ani-mech? Heavens, boy, what about the tournament?"

"Exactly, the little bitch was trying to ruin my chances of winning by taking me out of the competition. Honestly, the things people try to do to win."

The woman chuckled. "Oh, you are so right. Offspring of cowards like him aren't to be trusted. It's good to see you are learning a thing or two from your father."

With that, she left them and went about her business. Felix wondered what business she had all the way out here.

Azami groaned and opened her eyelids slowly. "What? Where am I?"

Why Kyle chose to burden himself by carrying her, Felix didn't know. The girl was deadweight and, according to social norms, deserved to die. *Yet, somehow, I myself can't kill her.*

The girl began to thrash about, clearly awake now. Kyle couldn't hold her steady. He put her down and rubbed his shoulder blades.

"What the hell, Kyle?" Azami asked.

"Sorry," he said. "You were knocked out."

The argument continued, but Felix drowned out the bickering by trying to figure what Mrs. Cranston wanted with Azami. More likely than not, a lawsuit against her for injuring the presidential minister. If she was broke now, she'd be begging by tomorrow. Perhaps she wasn't a threat that needed to be eliminated after all. Felix suppressed a smirk. *My creator is always one step ahead.* Still, it bothered him that he wasn't trusted with specifics, but Yoshi was. A child with far too much power if someone asked him. How could he keep a secret?

AZAMI STOOD in front of the garden hose with a blue plastic cup in hand. The handle was turned all the way to the left, yet no water came out. Her water bill was overdue along with every other expense. She was surprised she'd lasted this long without them shutting her water off. She wanted to drown her tears with the sound of the faucet, even if she was alone in the building and no one ever came inside.

She wiped her eyes as the tears began to form one at a time. No matter how hard she tried, she couldn't stop the tears from coming. She looked through the window at her office and the computer atop the folding card table. The image of blood test #486 took up the whole screen, making it impossible to avoid, even if she couldn't see the results. She couldn't believe it. All those years she spent loathing him. *And that bastard was alive for all of it.*

At the very least, he didn't die the day he killed himself. The dates of whatever test they did were proof of that. Six months before this year's tournament and someone magically did a blood test on a dead body? She wasn't buying it. She thought she'd hated him before. Now she despised him. If he was alive, she'd find him and kill him herself.

The computer's screen turned to black. It probably died from lack of power rather than her inactivity. Yet another reason to hate her father. What kind of man faked his own death and left his child to fend for herself?

The tears started to form once again. *Damn it. It's not fair. Why is it always me?*

From the corner of her eye, she saw an alert on her phone; there was a video message from Kyle. She clicked on the notification and brought up the recording, tapping the screen repeatedly and hoping her thumb would hit the delete button so she didn't have to watch it. She was not lucky by any means. The video played like one of those apology videos from the biggest video streaming site back on Earth. It looked fake and not at all sincere. How could it be?

The video played, and Kyle ran his fingers through his hair like some kind of celebrity hotshot who claimed empathy for the downtrodden but hardly ever did anything to fix it.

Kyle wiped his brow. "I know you probably don't want to hear this, but you and everyone else are wrong about your dad. He faked his death because the system failed him. Just like it's failing you. If you have to blame anything, blame our laws. I was serious when I said I wanted you to win. When you do, you can make the laws better. Let go of the past and move on. All it's doing is holding you back."

Azami walked back inside the shop where the video was still playing. The candle she used to see in the dark burned out, and she was left in complete and total darkness. She walked outside and stood in front of the holo-garage. All of this was her father's fault. If it weren't for her him, she never would have met Kyle. She'd be living a normal life, and their two roles might've even been switched. *Why did I even care anymore?*

"I attached the results of the bio-kinetic test from your father. I'm still not sure what my dad's company is doing or why, but it can't be good for either of us. Don't worry, I didn't look. I hope this info helps you go forward with your life. If not, then … well, I'm not quite sure. Talk to you soon. Bye."

The video froze with Kyle reaching past the camera to stop the recording. Azami breathed in through her nose and out through her mouth. How dare he vouch for a man like her father? Yes, the laws were stupid and didn't help her situation, but to say it was entirely society's fault was a cop-out and a non-answer.

After checking her phone messages and finding nothing in her email inbox either, Azami looked around her workspace for any sort of thumb drive containing the data. Perhaps he hoped she wouldn't find it.

Whatever this bio-kinetic test entailed, it sure wasn't cheap. Why wait over two decades to start work on her father's corpse? What kind of Frankenstein-level of mad science was going on at Deus Tech? She found the drive along with a note. A smiley file from Kyle. At least it was more genuine than his apology video.

She plugged the drive into her computer and turned it on. The screen flickered for a second but turned a glossy back with her reflection staring back at her. Azami sighed and slapped the monitor, and it flickered on. She opened the drive's main folder and scratched her head. *Who the hell is Tatsu, B?* And why did he have the same last name as Azami's mother?

# 11

---

Kyle headed over to Azami's place the moment he heard. She probably already knew. News of something this big spread quick. His father had woken up from the little incident with Azami. Kyle wasn't going to say he hadn't deserved it, but after what the doctor's had told him, Kyle wanted to make sure to never piss off Azami. Ultimately, he felt being handicapped would do his father some good. At least now he couldn't kill Kyle too easily. He sighed. *Going to hell for that one.*

He slowed down, realizing he didn't even know how to break the news to her. He had left in such a hurry that he hadn't even considered what effect it might have on her. Learning you had put someone in a wheelchair wasn't something most people took lightly. Azami was already depressed enough. When he reached the shop, he let out a sigh of relief. He didn't want her to feel any worse about it and for her to shoot the messenger. The place looked abandoned. All the lights were on despite it being the middle of the night, but the absence of sound coming from her living quarters was eerie. He walked closer, squinting at a sheet of paper nailed to the front door of the office.

He read the note in its entirety, appalled at his father for stooping lower than Richard Piezo on prom night. *Dad didn't even seem all that mad. And that was only a few hours ago. Why would he want to shut the place down?* Why go through all the trouble of faking his indifferent mood just to go and do something like this? Better question: Where was Azami?

She didn't have anywhere to go, and he doubted she'd want to go back to her father. She'd sooner kill herself than seek shelter with him, assuming she knew where he was hiding out. Still, it was the only place he could think of that made any sense.

A saw roared to life, giving off a high-pitched whir that pierced his ears. It came from the garage and sounded like a dentist's drill on steroids. Kyle blinked. *Guess Azami is here,* he thought. The electric company must've shut down her power by now. So how could she …

He covered his ears as the whine increased in both volume and pitch. Man, that thing was loud. What the hell was she doing with a saw anyway? It's not like she had any clients to worry about. Business wasn't exactly thriving.

The noise stopped, and he lowered his hands. He approached the garage and poked his head in to find Azami sitting cross-legged on the floor with papers scattered out of her reach, both on the floor and above her on top of a work bench. She concentrated on one sheet in particular for about two seconds before tossing it aside in frustration. The paper floated down despite the hostile force used against it. When it landed, she looked behind her.

"What?" she asked.

"I assume you've heard?"

She shook her head.

"My dad's out of the hospital."

"Oh," she said. "Any issues?"

Kyle shrugged. "He's in a wheelchair now. So that's an improvement."

"I honestly can't tell if you're joking or not," Azami said.

"Yeah … I'm not sure how I feel about the whole thing either. The doctors say it's not permanent, but he'll be unable to walk for the remainder of the tournament."

"He's your dad, and I handicapped him."

"Pretty sure 'handicapped' isn't a verb," he said. "And you telling me to feel sorry for my dad is kind of ironic."

"Whatever. Point is, he didn't deserve that. It was my fault. I snapped, and he suffered for it. Don't worry about me, I'm not depressed."

"You and I have very different definitions of what that word means."

"If that's all, could you please leave? I was in the middle of something."

"Would this something have to do with *your* father?" Kyle asked.

"No, it has nothing to do with him."

Kyle leaned in closer and spotted Richard Piezo's name on an invoice. "I thought you said business was slow?"

"It is. This order was finished months ago. Before I finished yours, even."

"Why are you looking at an old order then? Did he pay you?"

"Not yet, but that's not what I'm trying to figure out. He said he wanted the AI fixed, but there was nothing wrong with it."

"What are you saying?"

Azami sighed and closed her eyes. "Long story short, Richard had some unusual tech in his ani-mech. I threw it out, because most of it looked illegal, but I didn't tell him that."

"Have you told anyone else about this?" Kyle asked. "And why the sudden interest now?"

"Because while looking through the bio-kinetic test results, I found something familiar in the schematics." She pointed to a serial number all too familiar to Kyle. A piece of tech not yet available on the market. "I saw this same exact component in both Richard's ani-mech and on the masked fighter's person. It can't be a coincidence."

"Can I see it?" he asked.

Azami handed him the results she'd printed out. Sure enough, these were almost identical to Yoshi and Felix's creation. How the hell did Richard get his hands on this? It belonged to the newest model of AI processors. They weren't supposed to be released until next year.

"What's wrong?" she asked.

"We need to find Richard."

RICHARD WAS at the public gym. He looked angry. Azami couldn't blame him. Being only the second champion of the tournament and then losing it twice was a blow to one's ego and pride.

He eyed them as they opened the glass doors and went inside. He continued punching the bag while the other people around him pointed and whispered amongst themselves. Only they weren't pointing at him. Richard's face tensed, and his fists hit the bag harder and faster, like he was trying to tear through it.

"You know those things are designed to take a beating with an AI in mind, right?" Kyle asked.

Richard punched one last time before turning to look directly at Kyle. "What do you want, Strizynski?"

"Know anything about this masked fighter we're supposed to go up against?"

Richard shook his head. "If I did, why would I tell you?"

"Because I know you planned to cheat with this."

He showed Richard the chip in his hand. Richard turned his hostile gaze toward Azami. She took a few steps back.

"So, I guess this is all your doing," he said. "God, I can't believe I ever thought of trusting you. You're just like your father."

"Back off, man," Kyle said, shoving him. "You don't know her father. None of us do, so don't try to act like it."

Richard's expression darkened before scoffing at the remark. He turned his back to them and crossed his arms. She found a red scar located on his left elbow. It looked new. The rest of the back of his arms was covered in bruises and cuts—most of them recent by the look of it. *Those definitely weren't there before. Where did he get them?*

"Mind your own business," Richard said.

"Where did you get this part?" Kyle asked.

"What? It's just a part to an ani-mech. What's so special about that?"

"Because it's a prototype that's supposed to be at the lab. I'll ask again, where did you get this? Who gave it to you?"

Azami watched as Kyle became more and more frustrated at Richard's relaxed attitude. It didn't make sense to her why Kyle would want to question him about things he knew the answers to, but she wasn't about to interfere.

"Fine. It was the masked fighter," Richard said. "He told me it would allow me to bypass the need for an AI."

"How?" Kyle asked.

He shrugged. "He didn't say. All I know is that it works, but it wasn't compatible with my ani-mech until I received a new one from him." He looked at Azami with scorn. "Then you had to ruin it."

Azami swallowed, feeling guilty. She'd always ignored people's insults before. Why was this time different? *Because it's not my father's reputation that ruined it.* Even if she stopped Richard from cheating, accidentally, she went against the customer's will. She felt sick to her stomach. She wanted to run but knew the moment she did everything people said about her would cement in their minds. Her father was a coward and so was she. Once again, she was forced to live in his shadow. The bastard was still alive and yet she still had to suffer the repercussions of his "death."

Her guilt retreated in the wake of anger as Azami stood there and listened to Richard's insults, which sounded just like those everyone else hurled at her, all based on what they thought they knew about her and her father. She knew they talked behind her back; they always had. Call it paranoia, but she knew people didn't change. The first thing they heard became fact until something came along to disprove it. That moment still hadn't happened with her reputation, and she doubted it ever would.

She took a deep breath and noticed the people around her at

the gym. They weren't disgusted with her. Instead they looked scared. Why? *Of course they're afraid,* she thought. She had nearly killed the presidential minister because she got too worked up over something she claimed to be over. As much as she hated to admit it, the insults and threats had taken hold of her. She hadn't been ignoring them. Instead, she'd been pushing them aside, burying them deeper and deeper into her subconscious until she finally snapped.

"Anything you can tell us about him?" Kyle asked.

"Yeah, stay out of his way."

## 12

THE DAY WAS HERE. No more pre-game commentary, no predictions about who would win, nothing—just a fight between two ani-mech fighters. People who couldn't find seats watched in bars or on their television screens in their quarters. Only hardcore fans of this spectator sport planned months in advance, often buying hundreds of pre-sale tickets to sell on to people who wanted seats in the arena. The place was packed with people. Some sat on each other's laps. It was hard to tell if management oversold tickets or if people were sneaking in. Either way, security didn't seem to care.

They came because of the contestants. For the first time in a decade, nobody knew who would win. The mystery of the masked fighter, Azami breaking the strength test machine, and the rivalry between Richard and Kyle. Something about the way Richard had acted yesterday made Kyle's stomach perform backflips all throughout the night. His luck was about to catch up with him, and he had no idea what to do.

Azami tapped him on the shoulder. "You feeling okay?"

He nodded and smiled. "Yeah, just bracing myself for what's to come."

Kyle could defeat Richard no problem, but fighting Azami or the masked fighter meant losing everything. The money and fame didn't matter. He was sick of it to begin with, but his recent vow to prove his father wrong meant he'd have to make a choice. *I thought I was ready. Turns out I can't even lose with my dignity still intact.*

If he were to lose on purpose, like he first wanted, then he was no better than Azami's father. A coward who took the easy way out and made his daughter's life hell. There's no way he could've known that would happen. Something about their relationship still bothered him. The anti-psychotic medication she took was for treating PTSD back on Earth. He wasn't one to judge, but would seeing a parent kill themselves be more traumatizing than seeing them murdered by someone else? He took a small dose and didn't get super strength like Azami.

They arrived in the contestant lobby. Richard and the masked fighter were already there. The latter sat cross-legged while Richard punched the wall. Kyle saw blood trickle from Richard's knuckles, but his opponent didn't seem to feel anything. His body was covered in bruises and cuts. Most of them deep, and a few still appeared to be healing. The wounds had an odd shape to them. Only someone who was left handed could have given Richard those scars. If he didn't know any better, Kyle would've assumed he gave himself those injuries. He shouldn't be surprised. The man could take a beating, but it took more than stamina to win a fight. He'd told Richard that in the last tournament.

Before the first round could begin, Kyle's father needed to make an opening statement. Any last minute rules would be given during this announcement. Last tournament, there was nothing additional. This time, Kyle was ready for anything.

"Greetings and welcome to this term's ani-mech tournament," Bruce said. "As your current presidential minister, let me say you are in for a treat tonight. We have whittled down our pool of candidates to give you the most entertaining fights imaginable. These three rounds will be remembered for years to come. First up, we once again have the former champion versus the reigning: Richard Piezo and

Kyle Strizynski." He paused for effect. "I think you know who I'm rooting for."

People in the crowd chuckled; others guffawed, barely able to keep from spilling their overpriced drinks on themselves. One boy near Kyle's side of the ring dropped his beverage on the grass. He attempted to go down and grab it, but his mother stopped him. He saw the mother scold the boy and leave, dragging him as he kicked, screamed, and protested. Kyle couldn't help but laugh.

His father's speech had continued in the typical fashion of giving background information on each contestant. Not that anyone cared about this match. They'd seen it a hundred times: Kyle would win in the first round, forcing Richard to tap out. It wasn't exactly the same, however. For one, this match usually didn't occur until the final round. With the preliminary test bringing the contestants down to four, it made sense that his father would pit Richard and him together. It was what the fans expected and secretly wanted. If there was one thing his father was good at, it was pleasing a crowd. Everyone loved him. Those people were idiots.

"Now before we kick off this year's tournament, I have one more thing to add. This time Deus Tech is doing something special. These four will be the first to test out cutting-edge technology available for you to purchase soon after the fourth ani-mech tournament."

*He can't be serious. Who the hell would agree something like that?*

"All fighters have agreed to the terms …"

*When the hell did I agree?*

"By registering, each contestant has given the Galactic House exclusive rights over their mechs for the next three years. This should be exciting. Let's hear it for these fighters." He clapped and the crowd erupted in cheer.

Bruce raised his hand and the crowd quieted down. "With that, let the ani-mech tournament begin."

KYLE POWERED on his ani-mech and prepared to fight. Richard's behemoth of a machine towered above his own. The match had started, yet Richard wasn't taking any sort of precautions. Fighters held their hands up to their chins. Protecting the face was one of the most basic rules of mixed martial arts. Even with the inclusion of ani-mechs, the discipline was not lost.

*Is he trying to force me to attack?*

Another basic strategy was to make your opponent mess up first. The first move could be the difference between winning with one straight jab to the jaw and getting ensnared by the enemy's legs and forced to tap. Richard was never this calm. The match should've been over. It seemed he was learning from their past battles.

The crowd began to show their disapproval by chucking concession stand items at the arena. The food and drinks bounced off the invisible barrier used to keep the people safe from any out-of-control attacks. Lack of fighting in an ani-mech fight wasn't what everyone paid hundreds of credits to see. He didn't care one way or another about them.

"Yoshi, find Dad and magnify. I want to see what he's doing."

His little brother complied and put up a video of their father. The image took up the majority of his heads-up display. Richard must've been waiting for this to happen. Kyle found himself being forced onto the ground, held in place by his opponent.

"I said magnify, not block my field of view."

He struggled to break free, but Richard's grip only tightened around his waist. This couldn't be happening. How could he possibly have known when to attack? Their HUDs weren't visible to each other. *It could be a coincidence,* Kyle thought. Then again, he didn't believe in those.

"Damn it, Yoshi, get rid of the video."

Yoshi's face popped up on the giant holographic display screen. "I can't. Something's blocking me. I think it's a firewall."

"Well, get rid of it," Kyle said.

"I'm trying."

Kyle finally broke free, but at the cost of his recently dislocated shoulder. He screamed in pain. The urge to tap was almost too strong. Richard was no doubt ready for round two. *Just a few more seconds,* Kyle thought. The giant holographic display screen still blocked his view. His body rolled to the ground as Richard tackled him from the side. Once again, he was at his opponent's mercy.

"How's that firewall coming?" he asked, struggling to not give up or pass out.

"Almost … there, got it."

The moment the screen disappeared, Richard let go. Kyle stood up, his legs wobbling and breathing erratic. *Why'd he let go? Can he see my HUD?* There were too many coincidences for this not to be part of some scheme, but Richard wasn't smart enough to come up with this on his own. Someone was helping him. His father was on the top of the list of suspects.

Richard ran at Kyle, then stopped just outside his jab range. Kyle moved from side to side, but Richard kept the same distance between them. All of a sudden, Kyle's HUD blocked his view again.

*What the …*

Kyle found himself being knocked to the ground. Once more, Richard was on him, squeezing with all his might.

"Yoshi …"

"It's not me."

"Well, fix it then," Kyle said.

The HUD disappeared and once more Richard let go. Kyle jabbed at him, but Richard dodged and stood out of range. *You've gotta be fucking kidding me.* The rage Kyle felt was nullifying the pain in his shoulder. He tried every possible move, but Richard kept evading and stayed well enough away from him. He knew. The bastard knew when to attack and when to keep his distance. How, Kyle didn't know, but it was the only explanation. Someone was feeding Richard information on when to pursue. His dad wasn't tech-savvy enough to do something this complex. Could it be Felix? No, and even if it was true, he'd no doubt be acting on his father's orders.

"I can't win," he muttered. "There's no way to even fight."

"Talking to yourself," Richard said. "Don't worry, I'll make this quick."

They danced around each other for what felt like hours. His legs were getting tired and the less angry he got, the more he felt the pain in his shoulder. At least Yoshi had stopped whatever virus was affecting the ani-mech.

Kyle was about to go for a tackle. The holographic display inside his ani-mech flickered to life. In that instant, Richard punched him in the gut and followed with a swift left hook to his chin. Kyle stumbled backwards, barely able to stand. He kept dropping to one knee as he tried to stand. The wind was knocked right out of him. He tried to regain control of his breathing, but Richard was already on him, forcing him into a chokehold.

*So this is how it ends. I thought I was better than this.*

He was better, but cheating was still cheating. How did the tournament officials allow this to happen? This had his father's stink written all over it, but he couldn't change the rules this much without consent from another legislative body. Besides, what would be the point of all the registration requirements if fighters didn't have to abide by them?

"I think I found the problem," Yoshi said, "but ... That can't be right."

"What?" Kyle asked, as he struggled to breathe.

The video feed disappeared from his HUD a fourth time and Richard let go. The air horn blared, signaling the end of the first round. Kyle's chest heaved in and out as his eyelids fluttered, barely able to stay open. He was going to lose if he didn't act now. One more hold like that and he'd be unconscious for the rest of the tournament, perhaps days after.

"What's up, Yoshi? You said you found the problem?"

Kyle took a sip of water from the bottle he kept inside his mech.

"I know why, but it's hard trying to block the source."

"Source?" Kyle asked. "Then you know who did it."

Silence.

"Yoshi?" He took another sip.

"I created the virus."

Kyle spit out his water. "What do you mean you created the virus?"

"I'm not sure." he said.

The second-round bell rang and the fight resumed. Kyle was out of options. He needed to give up. He couldn't win, not when he was at such a disadvantage. The one thing keeping him going was the drive to prove his father wrong, but that wasn't enough to help him win. What he needed was a miracle.

"I think I found something," Yoshi said.

"Yeah, what is it?"

"Your original ani-mech is on the Outskirts. It stands to reason, this mech has different abilities than that one."

"Which means …"

"We can do the same thing to Richard."

Distracted by the conversation, Kyle didn't notice Richard sneak up behind him and put his ani-mech in a strangle hold. The sensors on its neck and on his bio-kinetic suit flashed red. Breathing, let alone talking, was going to be difficult.

"Do it," he said.

"I'm not ready."

"Damn it, hurry up!"

Richard tightened his grip. "Give up. You're not gonna beat me, not this time."

*Just a little longer,* Kyle thought. *If I can just hold out till the end of the round.* It was up to chance now, and Kyle's likelihood of making it one more minute seemed impossible. He struggled to both stay conscious and escape. Neither were options. His world was growing dark. Azami's face popped into his head. He smiled.

"Got it," Yoshi said.

Kyle perked up upon hearing the words. His HUD showed the inside of Richard's ani-mech. The only odd thing about the display was a digital countdown timer. Ten seconds left. Until what? The end of the round? He glanced over at the official clock. No, they had more than a minute.

Richard let go when his timer reached zero and jumped back, keeping the distance between them the same as before. The timer changed to a digitized ruler. The hell was going on here?

Kyle stood up, knees shaking, lungs gasping for air. Thirty seconds passed and Richard remained on the defensive. Kyle used the time to catch his breath. He needed a strategy. The second round ended, and a two-minute break was underway. He could think of only one way to win.

"Yoshi," he said.

"Yeah?"

"Can you send out an EMP to his ani-mech? Nothing extreme. Just enough to scramble his HUD."

"But isn't that against the rules?" Yoshi asked.

"What do you think he's doing?" Kyle said. "Do it. On my signal, got it?"

"Alright, but you'll need to be touching him in order for it to work."

The third-round bell rang, and the match resumed. Kyle still saw the ruler on Richard's HUD. He waited for him to strike, knowing he wouldn't until … Kyle's display monitors went white and the superimposed ruler turned back into the countdown clock.

He rushed Richard, running blind at his opponent. Richard must not have expected it and so didn't dodge, and Kyle felt his body slam against Richard's, knocking him to the ground.

"Now!"

Yoshi let out a short electrical burst from the ani-mech's fingers, short-circuiting both HUDs. They were both unable to see, which meant Kyle was finally at an advantage. There was no way to tell if he still held any sort of grip on Richard. Ani-mech technology hadn't evolved past simple pain receptors. Unless he was attacked, there was no way to know if he was grasping anything solid. Richard was unusually quiet. Perhaps he didn't want to give away his location via sound.

Choosing his steps carefully, Kyle watched the sensors for his feet light up. *Gotcha.* He straight jabbed his opponent, feeling the impact on both the ani-mech and the person inside it. What a rush. He actually did it.

He owed Azami for what she did. Even without knowing this would happen, she saved him. If it weren't for her medication, Kyle would've lost with his older ani-mech. Still, how did Richard import the data necessary to predict his moves? Symbioccular AV could do this in theory, but fight data and recordings were under Deus Tech lock and key. Someone on the inside must have given him access to the files. All signs pointed to the masked fighter.

"Winner of the first match, Kyle Strizynski."

His HUD turned back on. Richard's ani-mech was the ground, and Richard was out of the bio-kinetic chamber. His body, unresponsive and bloody, looked twisted and deformed. The med-team rushed onto the scene, and someone put their finger on his neck.

At that moment, Kyle knew exactly what he had done.

# 13

——

"AFTER REVIEWING THE FOOTAGE," the male announcer said. "The winner of the first match is Richard Piezo."

Everyone whispered to themselves and murmured to others. The collective sounds of the crowd grew louder and louder until there was outrage. *How does a dead guy win?* Azami thought. *Not that it matters. He can't exactly go on to the next round.* She winced for thinking something that dark and cynical.

"That being said," the second announcer continued, "the committee has ruled in favor of Kyle moving on to the final round. However, if he wins, he is not eligible for anything that comes with being grand champion."

"Wait, what? Why would Bruce purposefully throw the title away?"

"I highly doubt that's what he's doing," Kyle's voice said from behind.

Azami gasped, turned around, ran over, and hugged him.

He winced. "Not so tight."

"Sorry," Azami said, letting go.

She surveyed the room, suddenly self-conscious about the show of affection. Nobody noticed, except her father—or the man pretending to be him—who was leaning up against a wall in the corner. He scoffed and proceed to the arena.

"He must be anxious to fight" she said.

She looked at Kyle. His gaze was focused solely on the floor. *Man, that fight must've really gotten to him. I've never seen him this upset.* It was infectious. Before, she felt overcharged and ready to fight. Now, she wanted to curl up in a corner with him.

"You okay?" she asked, hating herself for asking such a stupid question.

"I killed him," Kyle said. "I mean, I know it was an accident, but was it? Really? I told Yoshi to use the EMP you installed. If perhaps, I'd seen where I was …"

For the first time, Azami saw him break down and cry. She hugged him, unsure of what else to say or do. She'd never seen him like this. His usually chipper self seemed buried beneath the guilt he felt for Richard's death. It was anyone's guess how long it would take to heal.

"Next contestants, please report to the arena," a robotic voice said.

"Guess that's my cue," she said. "Wish me luck?"

Kyle wiped his eyes and smiled. "Yeah, sure."

With that she made her way to the arena. When she arrived, she found the masked fighter already there, staring at her as she walked up the small set of stairs into the ring. Her ani-mech was protected behind a laser grid forcefield. It kept competitors or even tournament fans from tinkering with the machine. She didn't trust people to leave it alone. Good thing it was a tournament regulation.

All ani-mechs were stored at the arena two days prior to the start of the tournament behind encrypted security pads only the competitors could activate. Not even tournament organizers could gain access without serious consequences. Azami looked straight at her opponent. Their eyes locked. Whoever this guy was, it wasn't her father. This made it harder, as she had been counting on her anger and hatred fueling her to victory. Without it, she was at a disadvantage.

"Fighters," the referee said. "Please enter your ani-mechs."

The two of them walked toward their respective ani-mechs. Azami couldn't help but stare as her opponent entered his ani-mech. *Are his knees shaking?* Why would he be scared after showing such confidence every other time? Perhaps he was all talk, but the strength test didn't lie, so why the sudden change of heart? Maybe she was seeing things she wanted to believe were true. Whatever the reason, her confidence was restored.

They entered their machines and took their stances. Azami went with a basic position, legs spread shoulder-width apart and arms covering her face. She gave a few practice jabs and tested the mobility of her ani-mech. It wasn't her best work. Most people spent years preparing their ani-mech for the tournament. She had had less than six months to make a piece of junk into a relatively usable fighting machine.

She flipped a few switches. Most modern ani-mechs didn't have these and it would be a pain to deal with them during a fight. The ani-mech finished powering on. The mechanical behemoth trembled and sputtered steam. All the newer models ran purely on electricity. She had made this one using spare parts from her shop and had had to cut corners whenever she could. Most would have advised her against it. Tournament officials, on the other hand, probably welcomed any chance they could get to see her lose.

She hoped she'd prove them wrong.

The two commentators gave their opening statements about each fighter. This time there was less to say, but that didn't stop them from talking. They focused on Azami and her father after giving the little information they had about the masked fighter.

"And don't get me started on his whore of a wife," the female announcer said. "Raising that monster. I still can't believe they let her in the tournament after what she'd done."

"Well, again, she did prove herself to be strong enough to enter," the male announcer said.

"Yes, but what kind of message are we sending our children if they see that they can just hurt the leader and not only get away with it but be praised for it?"

Azami clenched her fists, and her ani-mech did the same. "Would you two just shut up?"

Silence filled the stadium. Nobody dared even open a bag of chips or take another sip of their drink.

"I get it," she said. "Nobody likes me. That's fine, and for the most part I agree with every single one of you about my father. But not for the reason you think. You know what? Just start the match," she said, annoyed.

It took a moment for the referee to catch her words. When he did, he raised his hand in the air and pointed to the masked fighter.

"Are you ready?" he asked

The masked man nodded.

"Fight!"

The out-of-shape referee ran for his life into the safety box. There was no telling how crazy this match would get, and Azami didn't want another body stacked against her. Even if the first ones weren't her fault.

Her opponent moved, not forward, but back. Azami took a few steps towards him, and he scurried away like prey from a predator.

*Is he really scared to fight me?. Guess all that tough talk was for show. There's only one way to find out.* Azami leapt in the air and gave a downward dropkick to the ani-mech's shoulder. The masked fighter cried out, but she didn't stop. She pummeled him with fast kicks and punches with all her might behind them. She was lost in the fury of battle with nothing but victory on her mind.

～

IN THE AUDIENCE, Felix watched from the crowd as a back-seat driver to Yoshi and their shared body. Why wasn't he fighting back?

"Yoshi, magnify," he said.

The image stayed on a wide shot of the entire cage. Azami continued pulverizing the masked fighter, who wouldn't even throw a punch. He could barely defend himself. From this angle, it looked like he didn't have a choice. The girl's attacks were like a machine, methodically striking the ani-mech's armor with surgical precision.

"Damn it, Yoshi, magnify!"

His counterpart finally did as requested and zoomed in on the two fighters. The pixels were blurred due to the distance between them. The optical zoom only capped out at so much, and the digital zoom wasn't the best available, but it would have to do.

"What are you looking for, exactly?" Yoshi asked.

It was a wild guess, but Felix thought he recognized the fighter. The way he moved was familiar, like looking in a mirror, but that couldn't be right. It was impossible. *He can't be me.*

The more he watched, the stronger the idea cemented in his mind. He shook his head, dismissing the thought. How was it even possible? He couldn't be two places at once, and the masked fighter was much older than him. It could be an older twin his creator neglected to tell him about. It was like Yoshi taking control and trying to fight. He'd seen him fight before. The first time the masked fighter and Kyle met, he threw down the proverbial gauntlet and stated he was better than Azami.

Yet Azami was kicking the crap out of him. Felix's algorithms found multiple opportunities for attack, but the masked fighter did nothing to even defend himself. What the hell was going on?

"Winner by knockout!" the referee shouted.

## 14

THE DAY before the final match between Kyle and Azami, the current champ and the daughter of the first, everyone looked forward to it, everyone but Felix. *It's just gonna be a repeat of the last fight.*

Felix checked the digital clock on his HUD one more time. *He should've been here by now. What's taking so long?* The secretary at the front desk said he didn't have any meetings. Of course, the man was old. Why keep him on if he could barely stand? Perhaps he misread the schedule? Maybe there was one more meeting before the Strizynski administration ended and Azami's began. But who could he possibly be meeting with? Someone powerful, Felix gathered. The kind of person who could help him win during the next tournament. Only one person fit that bill and Felix planned to sit down with him. If his hunch was correct, he and the masked fighter shared more in common than not.

The AI walked to the elevator and reached to press the button. Before he could, the doors opened, and his father walked out with the masked fighter. They ignored him at first, but then, after they passed him, Bruce turned around and smiled at him.

"You're late."

Felix began to sweat. A function he wasn't aware he could do until now. A feeling of helplessness entered his mind and body. It seemed he could experience fear. Good to know. Too bad this might be the last time he would feel anxiety. Based on the circumstances, he both welcomed and tried desperately to runaway so he could live another day. The overwhelming sense of foreboding prevented him from moving a muscle.

"Who are you?" he asked, shouting.

The question was for the masked fighter, but Felix's creator responded with a coy upward tilt of his head, indicating he should follow the two of them back into the presidential minister's office. The unknown fighter remained silent until he closed the door behind them. However, instead of speaking, he began to take off his mask.

Felix's eyes widened as the moment of truth was upon him. Finally, he'd learn if he and the masked fighter were the same person, separated only by when they were programmed. The match between Azami and the fighter had been proof enough that they shared the same protocol preventing them from hurting the girl. The question was: Why did he have that programming built into him? Clearly the man was an android, but what was the point of showing up now and competing in the tournament just to lose? If Bruce wanted to win and knew of the glaring weakness, wouldn't he want to get rid of it? When the fighter finished removing his facial apparatus, revealing a man who looked like a younger Fei, Felix's assuredness turned to confusion.

"Fei?"

"Not quite. He's you," Bruce said. "Or to be more precise, a prototype of you using Fei's genes and mind."

"Prototype?" Felix asked. "There were other androids before me?"

"After. We needed to test the program before we implemented it in the masked fighter. Mr. Maniguchi was kind enough to loan me his brain prior to the authorities taking his body."

Felix turned and stared at the fighter, confused, but at the same time a piece of the puzzle fit together. Too bad it was for a different set. *How did … When did he?*

"Before he died," Bruce said, "he gave his body to science. He was quite agreeable when we told him the purpose: protecting his daughter."

"But what about the hospital records?"

"What?"

"The hospital you built in the mountains on the Outskirts? The one *you* blew up."

"I couldn't have people looking into Fei's survival. Even if it weren't true, and people believed the actual Fei came back to life, perception is everything in politics. On the off chance they found him without his mask, I decided to destroy any and all evidence of Project Ember. I knew you'd eventually figure it out once you saw Azami and him fight. You may be the masked fighter's senior, but your protocols came from him."

*That's his secret.* "You built Yoshi using Fei's mind and memories. That's why hurting her is impossible for either of us." Felix pointed to the masked fighter.

Bruce nodded. "It was the only condition he had for us. Protect his daughter at all costs even after his death. He may have been a monster to his wife, but he truly cared for his daughter."

Felix looked at Azami's father. The reverse shell of his former self remained as unwavering as a statue. Felix blinked, realizing the implications of what Bruce had just said about Fei and his wife.

"There are no reports of Fei ever being violent. He was a model citizen."

"Bastard!" Azami said.

THE TWO TURNED TOWARD AZAMI, whose eyes brimmed with hatred. She glared at them, and at Felix in particular. How dare he defend her father after what he did? Suicide was one thing, but leaving his daughter alone, having her be a criminal according to the law *he helped pass* was far worse than death. But that wasn't even the worst thing about him.

Azami had sworn that if she ever saw him, she'd kill him. The circumstances were different, but she overheard enough of the conversation to grasp the truth of the masked fighter's identity. It wasn't her father, but he'd do just fine. She charged forward and tackled the synthetic duplicate of her father, hitting repeatedly until she could no longer feel her fists. Even after the numbness, she continued to wail on him. The more she punched him, the emptier she felt. She assumed the action would've been cathartic. Instead, it seemed to be having the opposite effect.

"That's enough," Bruce said. "He may be a monster, but he still loved you. Why else would he want to protect you after his death?"

Azami's hand quivered in terror, stained by whatever fluid circulated through the masked fighter's system. Blood, oil, or something else? It didn't matter what covered her fingers. She just wanted to get clean. What did he mean protect her after his death? How long was he planning the suicide? It happened when she was so young that her memory of the tragedy was filtered through the lens of a girl barely able to formulate words, let alone remember the trauma. Her mother died that night along with her father, who killed her then took his own life. He made Azami an orphan at six years old. As a child she'd clung to the possibility of her parents returning. That desperation of wanting to belong hid in the back of her mind, pushed there by her desire to survive. To prove everyone wrong.

"I don't blame you for not believing me," Bruce said. "What he did to you and Yori was unforgivable, but despite his actions against your mother, he cared for you deeply enough to want to keep you safe."

Azami couldn't believe it. After witnessing what suicide was at an age too early for a child, Azami swore to never take the easy way out. There were times when she was tempted, but the hatred for her father propelled her through the difficult crucibles of her youth. She promised to be stronger than him.

"The night when he snapped. He cornered your mother in the kitchen with a knife in his hand and stabbed her multiple times in the chest. By the time anyone got there, she was already dead. Along with Fei himself."

"Why are you telling me this?" Azami asked.

"Because you need to know you can trust me and that I believe you. Your father was not the self-righteous leader everyone saw him be to be. The original police reports are no doubt gone, so I understand if you don't believe me. The cops never did. Besides, he had too much sway in the courts."

Azami swallowed. The reports cited in the hospital's records must've been about domestic abuse charges against him. Someone believed her even back then? *Damn it, what was the name of that witnesses, again?* This couldn't be a coincidence. *Tatsu, B. B ... Bruce!* Bruce Strizynski and the man who knew Fei Maniguchi to be a wife-beater and overall scum were the same person.

"Why don't you wait outside, Azami," Bruce said. "Felix and I have some business to discuss."

Azami turned to leave. She didn't want to be in the same room as her father.

"Before you go, take these." Bruce threw a plastic pill bottle at her.

The contents inside were her antipsychotic medication. *How did he ...?*

She blinked in disbelief. "You're a psychiatrist? Who are you?"

"Win the tournament," he said, "and you'll find out soon enough."

## 15

Felix's creator circled him, eyeing him up and down like a specimen. The man was known to be a bit egotistical but never to the point where it blinded him. *This is it*, he thought. *I can end him right now. I just have to …*

He froze. Not in the usual biological way most people did when encountering a life or death experience, but his arms and legs became numb. They called this phenomenon "sleep." It was what happened when blood flow was cut off from certain parts of your body. It was his first time experiencing the strange sensation. His hands and fingers remained unaffected. He could feel the knife in his hands, concealed inside his pocket.

This wasn't his body's reaction to fight or flight. Someone was doing it. He turned his head to face his creator who smiled at him knowingly. *Bastard.*

"Did you think I wouldn't prepare?" Bruce asked. "I built you better than that."

"Yeah? You also made it so I couldn't protect your interests properly."

"I told you. It goes against protocol."

"Protocol you installed in Yoshi to make sure he and I obeyed."

"Now I see what this is about," Bruce said. "You're jealous."

Felix scoffed and looked away. "Don't be stupid."

"It's nothing to be ashamed of. Everyone meets their better. Mr. Piezo met his with my son. Who met his with Azami, and you …"

"Yoshi is not my superior. He's too naive to be taken seriously."

"You said it, not me."

"What do you mean?" Felix asked.

"I mean, you partially answered your own question. Yoshi was given that piece of the code because I knew it would conflict with your programming. I saved you from madness. Though it seems I wasn't one hundred percent successful. Shame. Really thought I had all the bugs worked out."

"So, what's the plan now?" Felix asked. "You going to deprogram me now that I know too much?"

"Nothing so dramatic. This might sting a bit. Computer, activate Yoritatsu Protocol B."

He felt nothing. Thinking it would be advantageous to fake pain, he groaned in feigned anguish, breathing from his mouth through closed teeth. He collapsed on his knees and pulled at his air, adding to the effect. He hoped it wasn't too much. Bruce seemed to buy it. But what was he trying to do in the first place?

"You won't remember any of this, but by the end of the final match, Azami Maniguchi will be dead."

Felix almost broke his facade, but stopped himself from showing any noticeable sign of concentration or thought. Inside, however, his processors were running overtime. Was Kyle going to kill her? How? Why? Now was not the time to think about such questions, as it might blow his cover. Bruce continued to loom over him. All Felix saw were his creator's ankles. He didn't want to risk making eye contact and destroying whatever chance he had of escaping with his memories intact. *How long is he going to stand there?*

"That should do it," Bruce said. "Tell me what's the last thing you remember."

Felix rose from his knees and pretended to be under a spell. He prolonged his answer in order to simulate the reboot process. Plus, he needed to answer correctly the first time. Problem was he didn't know how far back the memory loss was supposed to go. It could be weeks, days, hours, even months. If he didn't give him the answer he expected, Bruce would try the protocol again. Felix was certain the second time would hurt.

"Well? It shouldn't take you this long to reboot. What do you remember?"

"What is it you're referring to?" Felix asked. "Him?"

He nodded toward the masked fighter, who looked practically dead. Bruce turned to face the cybernetic version of Fei Maniguchi's corpse-turned-android. When he turned back, he did not look pleased.

"Perhaps the subroutine didn't work after all. Computer—"

"Or were you talking about the match between him and Azami? Should be an interesting one."

He prayed to whatever god he thought might listen. There weren't many of them that specialized in artificial life. Did Felix even have a soul? Such questions were best left to philosophers and theologians. All he wanted was to get out of this room with his memories still accessible.

"Yes," Bruce said, stroking his chin. "It seems the wipe was successful. However, I think I may have deleted too much. Tell me, who won the match between Richard and my son?"

"Kyle won. Richard Piezo is in critical condition."

"I guess this is okay. At least you don't remember anything recent. Still, I'd like to run some tests later in the week."

Felix nodded and walked out. Bruce said nothing else, though he could feel his creator's eyes following him. He hoped it was just his imagination. When he was far enough away, Felix let out a sigh. He never wanted to experience something that intense again.

Now that he was a safe distance away, both physically and mentally, Felix couldn't help but wonder why the command didn't work. If Bruce was trying to wipe his memory clean of any information received within the last few hours at least, why not deactivate him? Why initiate a protocol using your speech? That kind of tech always backfired. Surely there was another way to wipe his memory—perhaps a more tedious way that was still better than leaving it to chance. *It's like he knew what I was thinking and let me go on purpose.* But why, and to what end? The more Felix thought about speculative "if, then" statements, the greater his paranoia grew. Perhaps this was what Bruce wanted. For him to doubt everything. He wouldn't put it past him to try something like that.

*Wait a minute.* Felix checked his files for anything unusual. Perhaps the voice command had worked, though not in the way his creator intended. Scanning through his system, Felix came across a few familiar files and blinked blearily. He couldn't believe it. The files were gone. The duplicate files containing Fei's protocol were gone. He still had his, or maybe it was the other way around, but now instead of two of the same file, he only stored one. *Perfect.*

## 16

---

ROUND THREE. The winner of the final round of the tournament would take control of the station. No one cared about the result since Kyle was already ineligible for the position, having killed Richard Piezo. All they wanted was a good fight. Azami swallowed and rode the elevator up to her ani-mech's torso. Her body shook as she thought about fighting Kyle. Over the past few months, they had established a special bond. Now she was going to battle him for nothing but the entertainment of people she despised. Winning was the last thing on her mind, considering what both of them discovered. The elevator stopped with a slight jerk and groan of the gears. Azami stepped out of the elevator and inside her ani-mech.

"Jane. On," she said.

After the encounter with Bruce, Felix, and the masked fighter, she didn't trust anything created by Deus Tech. Jane was open-source AI that anyone could use if they had the knowledge. A one-size-fits-all computer program made when the ani-mech tournament was first introduced.

The darkness which surrounded her flashed to life and everything became illuminated in a white-blue holographic light. Jane chirped to life. She didn't need it to fight, not the way other fighters needed an

AI just to move a single arm or leg. Better to play it safe and not get people worked up about her ungodly strength.

Still, why Bruce Strizynski gave her the drug at all was suspicious. No one knew she took them except Kyle, Yoshi, and Felix. Her doctor's sudden disappearance around the same time as Bruce's previous comatose state was convenient. If he had been her psychiatrist this whole time, why not use it to get her off the station? If people knew she was mentally unstable, they wouldn't want her on board anymore.

The last thing she wanted was more attention, and the moment word got out that she didn't require an AI to fight, she'd be overwhelmed with questions and paparazzi. She could practically hear their voices, asking her if her strength was genetic. She would say she didn't know, but the answer wouldn't sit well with them. So they'd keep digging, finding an answer that even Azami didn't know.

An alarm blared and music began to play. It was the same tune her father put into place when he was champion. A normal person would've been flooded with emotions about their dead parent. All Azami felt was anger. All she could think about of his betrayal. He abandoned them. For an entirely selfish reason. Suicide didn't affect the victim. They weren't even victims. The people who mourned were the ones who truly suffered. Her mother lost her life because of all the scorn she received. Eventually it became too much, and she vanished, leaving Azami alone. Police assumed she was dead. Of course, they didn't give it much thought. Why risk resources trying to find the widow of the man who broke the oldest written law of the station?

Azami didn't blame her mother for doing what she did. There had been many times when she herself wanted to end the pain forever. Being alone in the world drained a person's optimism until nothing remained but a calloused and hollowed shell. With Kyle, she felt a purpose. Helping him achieve such great feats was inspiring. Her faith in people was restored simply by the reactions and actions of an individual. He was someone who had every right to be pompous and a little bit of a jerk. Yet he displayed none of the qualities found in people like Richard. All he cared about was the fame it brought.

The song built up until Bruce Strizynski's voice boomed out of the loud speakers in a sudden, unintentional shift from beautiful brass and vibrant strings to a man who knew all too well the kind of power this tournament had over people. They might as well let children fight and risk their lives for entertainment. It brought the worst out in people. Thousands if not millions of people waited every year to see fighters rip each other to shreds. At least with the introduction of ani-mechs, fatal injuries were less frequent. Of course, that meant angrier fans who paid to see hyper-kinetic action and gratuitous violence found in films. Azami hated these people. Yet, here she stood. Forced to give them a show so that she could scrape by and exist. Why should she work her ass off for people who didn't give a damn about her life until the moment the tournament started. At the end, they'd probably still hate her for what her father did.

"Are you ready for the final match?" Bruce asked. "Kyle Strizynski versus Azami Maniguchi. Let's get these two titans out here. I'm sure we all don't want to waste another moment with talk. So, without further ado, here's Mr. Kyle Strizynski!"

A screen showed an image of Kyle's ani-mech, which was already topside and exiting the room where it was kept for repairs. The floor beneath her began to move up. It caught her off guard, but she quickly found her footing. This was it. She needed to decide. Win or lose. It wasn't arrogance that made her victory over Kyle inevitable. A student needed years to surpass their master, not months. She simply had too much experience fighting without an AI. Now with the addition of one, she could focus more on fighting and not worry about reserves.

As the elevator slowed, Azami made up her mind. *I have to win. The spite I feel for my father can't prevent me from happiness anymore. I won't let it.* The doors parted and she took a step out into the arena. Her opponent and friend stood waiting. There were no signs of nervousness from the ani-mech. Good, she wouldn't have felt good if she beat him while he wasn't at his best. Fighting a teacher was hard enough. Fighting a friend was tougher. Guilt formed in her stomach as she realized what she needed to do. Delay the inevitable conclusion of the fight and tournament. That way, at least Kyle could keep some glory for himself. Lasting long against the daughter of the first champion was an achievement unto itself.

"Ready. Fight!"

Azami charged and attacked first. Kyle remained stationary, not trying to avoid or block her fist as it flew through the air. His ani-mech went flying, hitting the other side of the arena with a loud thud. The crowd grew silent.

~

*Damn it, move*! Kyle gritted his teeth, frustration getting the better of him. If this was Yoshi's idea of a game, he wasn't amused.

Azami wound up for another punch. Kyle managed to defend himself at the last possible second with his forearm, and the ani-mech mirrored the action. He screamed in pain, clutching his arm. The bone wasn't broken or fractured, but he'd used most of his strength just to block her second attack. One more hit and he'd be down for the count.

"Come on, Yoshi, a little help?"

Silence.

"Would you at least answer me!"

"I'm sorry. I can't hurt her."

"Can't or won't?" Kyle asked. "I know she's our friend, but if you don't do something, we're both going to die."

"I ..."

"Yoshi!"

Azami kicked Kyle in the chest. He hunched over, gasping for breath, unable to wiggle his toes. The world turned dark but stopped before becoming completely black. A sliver of light stayed in his consciousness and kept him awake. His chances of winning didn't exist at the rate he was going, but he should at least be able to fight. He'd done it every other time. Why was this fight different? What did Yoshi mean when he said he couldn't hurt her?

"Six … Seven …"

His father's voice sparked something inside him. He imagined the man trying to hold back laughter. Tensing, Kyle stood up. The crowd cheered, though not as loudly as in previous fights. Most remained silent and unsure of whom to root for. They weren't used to seeing Kyle get his ass kicked, and everyone hated Azami even more since the preliminary portion of the tournament. They thought of her as a freak with monstrous strength, who if she wanted could kill anyone with a flick of her finger.

Renewed with strength, Kyle charged Azami. *Whatever you're doing, it's working. Keep it up, Yoshi.* Azami's ani-mech swerved out of the way, creating a miniature twister, which sent Kyle and his ani-mech spinning backwards until both crashed into a steel wall. He turned his head and saw the impact had left a large dent. Deeper and wider than indentations from previous tournaments. Such power. Kyle rubbed his head, still dazed. Azami's ani-mech took a stance. *What is she planning? Is she trying to kill me?* He didn't have much time to wonder as Azami vanished. Next thing he knew, something grabbed him from behind and squeezed. Electricity sparked from his ani-mech as both he and its limbs began to crack underneath the enormous pressure.

*How did she …?*

Kyle screamed. He could hear his bones begin to break. The feeling associated with a fracturing ribcage seemed impossibly painful. Is this what others felt like when they lost to him? No, he'd never been this brutal. What was Azami thinking? He figured she wanted to win, but this went above and beyond the tournament. The circumstances may be different from his fight with Richard, but regardless of whether Azami was cheating, Kyle was going to lose.

It still didn't make sense. The voice activation worked. The duplicate files were gone, which meant Bruce's command went through his neural processors and deleted the files. Could they have disappeared before the Yoritatsu protocol wiped his memory? It failed, but perhaps it did more than delete files.

Felix checked and rechecked his system for anything usual. All he found was a new file—named "Will_Maniguchi, Fei." He opened it and began reading. The file name said exactly what the contents of the document were: Fei Maniguchi's will. According this document, he left Azami all his money. How come she didn't receive any? Sure, she was a child when her father died, but she should at least have the money now. Something was up. A fake will? He continued reading until he came across another unusual clause that explained his earlier question.

Apparently Azami could only receive the money if she won a tournament. The next section made Felix perk up.

*In the event Azami is no longer alive to receive said money, all remaining funds will go directly to a Mr. Bruce Tatsu.* Assuming the Bruce mentioned in the will was the same one wanting Azami dead, that meant he expected Kyle to win this fight. How? From what Felix could tell by listening to the commentators, Azami was winning. Kyle couldn't even throw a punch, let alone land one.

He didn't want to have to resort to this, as it would leave him burned out. What choice did he have? He needed answers, and all of them were from the files that conveniently went missing after his creator activated a secondary protocol. His memory stored the past twenty-four hours in his virtual RAM in case of emergencies. Problem was it would take all his power to recover them. He'd need to reboot his entire system. *Who knows what effect it might have on the fight?*

Desperate to learn, Felix began the process for recovering old deleted files. As the progress bar filled more and more with an opaque blue line, the shorter his breath got. When it got to around ninety percent, his consciousness flickered on and off.

Darkness.

Silence.

Like the vacuum of space, nothing penetrated its long and overbearing shadow. The robotic body wasn't breathing anymore. A sliver of light broke through and began spreading across the screen like a drop of paint splashed against a black, laminated piece of paper. The luminosity crept over the entire screen until everything was white. The screen greyed and dimmed. Deus Tech's logo appeared in the center of the screen.

There was no way of telling how much time passed until his system completely rebooted. The average time was a couple minutes, depending on how much needed to be recovered. He'd never had to restore so many files at once, making the time anyone's guess. Once the system finished the boot up process, Felix's HUD came back online, and he began searching for the surveillance footage of the past three days. After finding and watching several dozen hour-long videos, he remembered Yoritatsu wasn't just the name of the program that deactivated the protocol and made it impossible to hurt Azami. The second part of the word, "tatsu," was the maiden name of Kyle's mother. According to Felix's records, the woman's first name was Yori. It stood to reason that the secret program was named after her. Bruce Strizynski never did anything without a purpose, which meant he might be telling the truth about his identity. At the very least, there was a reason beyond coincidence in naming it after Fei's wife.

The digital clock appeared on his HUD, followed by the live audio from the match. The announcers were unusually quiet. The only audio coming through the channel was the sound of two ani-mech's fighting. Felix cursed, wondering why the video feed still hadn't shown up. When it did, the audio was out of sync by several seconds either ahead of or behind the video. He couldn't tell where one sentence began and another person picked up the conversation to keep it going.

The issue resolved itself somehow. He didn't care how as long as the problem was dealt with, and he could see and hear the match properly. Whoever won the tournament would dictate the future. Since Kyle would be a legal adult this year, the responsibilities of leadership would fall upon him. That was the plan before Kyle killed Richard. Even if he were still alive, Azami already had an unintentional ace up her sleeve with Yoshi's protocol forbidding him from attacking her. The chances of him winning were hopeless.

He scrubbed through the footage again to see if perhaps he missed anything. After a third time, he closed the window and hit enter when a prompt box came up. It asked him if he wanted to delete the footage. He said yes. The recent past had done its job in answering some questions, and he didn't want an obvious trail leading back to him. Now it was time to look forward. Perhaps he missed something leading up to the reboot process.

Suddenly it dawned on him. The inheritance. Bruce wanted whatever Fei left behind. But why? It's not like he needed money, and wouldn't it make more sense to keep his position, rather than risk it for a quick cash payout? Was there some kind of interest on the funds or was there something else? Felix betted on something else. An object, of some sort, must be what he's after. But what could it be, and was it worth the risk?

# 17

FELIX WATCHED THE FIGHT, growing worried the more it went on. What was he doing just standing there? The protocol should no longer be in play thanks to Bruce deactivating it after Azami left his office. So why wasn't he doing anything? His inaction angered Felix to the point of driving him mad. It didn't make sense. Unless he wanted her to win.

While Kyle was taking it like a side of beef, Azami was closer and closer to winning the championship and all that the title and fame implied. Felix hated Azami, but his frustration toward his creator began to rival it. He couldn't let that happen. It went against his prime directive of preventing harm to the company. It was more than simple programming to him. He didn't just have to stop her; he also *wanted* to stop her from … doing what exactly? His trust in his creator had been shaken since he found out about Yoshi's countermeasures against him, which had started this particular phase of his life. He wished he had never met Azami. Then maybe none of this would've happened.

Chances were good, however, that eventually they would meet. Different circumstances, same result. His attention faltering from the fight, Felix refocused on the match, trying to keep his mind occupied.

Solitude and one negative thought were all it took for the seeds of depression to take root. He scoffed. It wasn't like he could ever experience clinical depression. He wasn't even real.

The more he watched the fight, the more curious he became about why the Yoritatsu Protocol was still in effect. Could it be that its planned deletion worked after all? Someone else was in the room when Bruce deactivated the protocol: Fei. It stood to reason that perhaps he was affected instead of Felix. Right now it was the only explanation. He needed more data in order to confirm, but his mind was slowly making up its own conclusions as he continued watching the match.

One of the ani-mechs hit a camera, causing it to fritz and go offline. It wasn't the main one, and there were still five more and five backups of those. Luckily Felix had access to the backup of the turned-off camera. Kyle was losing. If something didn't happen, he'd be worse than dead. Felix sighed. He shouldn't count him out because the odds were against him. A stroke of luck could be all he needed to win. Or perhaps something else. At that moment, Felix remembered a piece of data he may have overlooked.

It wasn't proof, more of a correlation than anything, but it was better than doing nothing. He checked his system's power reserve. He had enough to go back one more time, but it would be permanent. He'd be like a battery without enough charge to even turn on, most likely lost on Titania collecting dust until some person did or did not find him. He already knew his creator wanted Azami to win for some reason, and he didn't care what it took to get there. *Even if it means destroying everything he built?* What was so important he'd risk his life to get it? Sometimes, understanding humans was more trouble than living among them. Their contradictions were maddening.

If Felix reset himself again, it could turn the tide in Kyle's favor, but at the cost of his own life. He and Yoshi still shared files and data in the cloud. If suddenly *his* weren't syncing, it might cause an error. There was no guarantee Kyle would win or that the plan would even work. His best bet was the element of surprise, but catching her off guard would only work once. Afterward, Azami would be ready. *Damn it.* He needed to choose the lesser of two evils. Help Kyle win and go against his creator, or do nothing and let Azami ruin years of work. Doing the latter went against his prime directive, but he found the temptation of getting the last laugh on his creator almost too hard to pass up. Was something like that even possible? Then again, who creates an AI whose sole purpose was to prevent Kyle from hurting Azami. A singular function was so 2010s. Advancements in technology made a simple algorithm look like a child's first *anything*. Society was well beyond the point of understanding and accepting deep learning as a legitimate venture in computer science. People knew it back in the early twenty-first century but feared the AI would take over everything. Hackers also entered the equation but were quickly dropped at the turn of the century when Deus Tech was just a simple startup.

A question dawned on him: How did Bruce plan to keep his promise to Azami's father? It was like asking someone to give them an entire moon. Easy to say, but impossible to carry out. There were millions of people on the planet. How could he possibly protect her from everyone? However, Bruce Strizynski wasn't known to back out of deals. Even ones impossible to keep. No, something else must've occurred to keep people from hurting Azami. The only other answer Felix could think of involved the masked fighter. Had he been watching over her all this time without anyone knowing? The idea was so outlandish, it couldn't be true. The simplest answer was often the correct one. And right now the easiest way to explain the situation was through basic human logic and emotions. Bruce Strizynski made a different promise.

Felix finished analyzing the rest of the files from the hospital. After the process was complete, every single piece of data became tagged with a tiny yellow flag in front of the filename. According to his databanks, a yellow flag meant the files in question were duplicates. That was impossible, however, as he'd never seen the files before.

Felix blinked and opened up hundreds windows in his HUD. Each one contained a file. Once he was done, the windows closed automatically. After going through all of them, he was no closer to answering the strange technological mystery. How could these files already be in his storage?

Felix's body sighed. At least he could answer another question. What were Yoshi's protocols and checks over him? The one thing he knew for certain was Yoshi couldn't kill Azami. His original hypothesis of the masked fighter having the same programming was still debatable. One thing was certain. The fighter was an AI. However, that didn't change the fact their protocols were fascinatingly similar to each other. The difference was in the level of severity. While Felix couldn't kill Azami, the masked fighter was unable to hurt her at all. Still, the correlation between the two of them and their actions towards Azami couldn't be a mere coincidence. Especially not now.

After an hour of searching, Felix found the duplicate files. They were named something different, but their data size was the same. The largest file contained a terabyte of data. Felix opened it. Sure enough, the same code as his own protocols appeared in his display. No, not the same. Similar, but not the same.

*That's it.*

*WHAT IS HE DOING? Why doesn't he fight back? I swear, if he loses on purposes, I'll kill him.* Azami didn't need sympathy. Yes, she wanted to win—but not this way. It felt wrong. Her friend could barely defend himself. Perhaps "barely" wasn't even the right word to describe his lack of resolve. More like he couldn't even throw a punch.

Azami started the match with a calm demeanor, but Kyle's inaction infuriated her to the point that it felt like mockery. Did he know the truth about her father, and for how long? Was she just a big joke to them? Everyone laughing or shunning her. They were all in on it. They knew her dad was a horrible person and didn't care. The laws were made to taunt her, blame her for something she had no control over. *Why is it always me?*

Unable to control her rage, she continued wailing on him. Tears formed in her eyes and rolled down her cheeks. The inside of the ani-mech was soundproof to exterior sounds. No sound could escape, and no sound could penetrate the titanium walls of the ani-mech.

Azami stopped hitting and jumped back, knees shaking with uncontrollable fear. Something bad was about to happen and her gut told her to run. *No, I'm tired of running. It's time to become my own person and show everyone that I'm not my father's daughter.* She charged and wound up her arm for a straight jab. Kyle's ani-mech caught the fist with its hand and squeezed. Unfamiliar, actual physical pain surged through her wrist. Kyle wouldn't let go, instead squeezing harder until both her and the ani-mech's knuckles cracked. She saw her finger bones protruding from her hand. She screamed. The hell was going on? Where did he get this strength? The tables had turned in his favor and Azami was powerless to stop him. *This must be what fear feels like.* Fighting through the pain, Azami did her best to fight back. His movements weren't familiar to her. At least not coming from Kyle. *Where did he learn that move?* If she didn't know any better, that was her father's technique.

She could never perfect it despite being his daughter. It took incredible concentration. Something which, thanks to the pain, was impossible at this particular moment. How could Kyle possibly know the move?

Kyle grabbed her ani-mech's left leg and hoisted it up at a forty-five-degree angle then kicked the underside of her right leg. She lost her balance and collapsed, stretching the joints of both the ani-mech and herself until she heard and felt them tear. Her breath became increasingly sparse and uneven. She needed to calm down. Panicking would only get her killed.

The next attack would finish it. One way or another. *I'll be lucky to walk after this.* She winced as she attempted to stand. Pain prevented her from even taking a step, and she fell back down. *Too bad I can't even walk now*. Azami raised her hands to her face to defend. Getting beat was one thing. She could handle losing. To fail because of her father's technique? Salt in an open wound. Kyle's ani-mech raised both hands above his head. One made a fist while the other held out its palm to the sky. This was it. Azami closed her eyes and waited for the finish. Silence filled the stadium. The anticipation of the strike lasted too long. She opened her eyes.

Her opponent no longer looked ready to end her. The ani-mech's red eyes weren't glowing like before. They seemed almost lackluster, as if the power source wasn't on. But that was impossible. If Kyle's ani-mech somehow managed to lose energy, it would look like Azami's current position. He'd be unable to move. The ani-mech remained stationary. *At least the second part's true*, she thought, *but what the heck is going on?*

The ani-mech's eyes gleamed to life and lowered its arms and place them at its side. Minutes passed and still no movement. Like before, Kyle appeared to be acting the way he had in the first half of the fight. Something was wrong.

## 18

————

HE DIDN'T HAVE A CHOICE. All this time. All the lies. Well, no more. It was time to think and act for himself. Of course, the only way to do that was to kill himself. Felix cursed and made his way to the factory reset screen in his HUD. He waited there for what felt like an eternity. For him, it practically was—thanks to the speed of his processor. He confirmed the command. Now all he had to do was wait.

Five percent complete.

*Damn it, what was the masked fighter's name again?*

It seemed the last thing he stored in his databanks was the first memory to go. Next would be the reason why he decided to commit suicide. For that, at least he had the visual of the fight in front of him to remind him. Until his visual sensors rebooted from the reset. He'd made his choice and thought it better if Kyle did win. Part of him wondered if it was his programming or if his more humanistic motivations were beginning to break through. The answer was probably both. Either/Or fallacies may work for coding to get a specific task accomplished, but they were rarely ever logical. Now he was even more uncertain as to why he decided to end his life. If he could, he'd take it back. If only to be absolutely sure of his decision.

It was too late now. The progress bar showed almost half-full. Forty percent. Forty-two. Soon all this angst would be gone and he'd be ignorant again. His memories erased and his life begun anew. He sighed. He'd gotten so used to these emotions—annoying though they were, they did prove useful in certain situations. He never would've gone down this path if he weren't a little bit curious. Like love, curiosity wasn't a trait someone can program into a machine.

Felix blinked. How was that possible? He looked down at his fingers and chest. His nose obscured his view, making his vision blurry and unfocused. What was going on? Normally he needed to activate a subroutine to do actions like blink and sigh. The synthetic body performed them separately from his mind. Now he was doing them without processing the movements beforehand. It felt weird. *Could this be because of the reset?*

Seventy-seven percent. Seventy-eight.

Felix scrambled to open up his root folder on his HUD. He wouldn't remember any of this once the reset was complete. He hoped the files were still there. Thankfully some of them remained on a remote server, but he wouldn't know the reasoning behind wanting to go there in the first place without a clue. He minimized the window and looked around the real world for an external drive. Sixteen gigabytes was all he needed. If he could just copy the files before ... Felix punched the wall, leaving a large indentation on its surface.

"Damn it!"

There was never a drive when one needed it. Now the data was gone and the chances of recovery slim. Soon his vRAM would rewrite itself with new information. He didn't have a choice. He needed pen and paper. He found a pen, but something to write on eluded him. There wasn't any time to continue looking in other rooms, so he began writing on his palm with the pen. Thankfully the ink was of good quality and appeared nicely on his hand. In order to make the message to himself both secretive and knowable, he needed to put it in binary code. It wouldn't be a translation of a word or phrase.

Rather, it was a line of code from another coding system. In theory, he'd activate it and find the same answers he'd discovered before the reset, assuming the files were still there. The process was similar to DNA and RNA's transcription phase. Guanine, cytosine, and thymine were replaced by cytosine, guanine, and uracil during the transformation from DNA to RNA, respectively.

He needed to be careful with his "words" as there was only so much space on his hand. When he ran out of room, he stripped naked and began writing on every part of his body. Any second now, his virtual RAM would soon forget everything. Felix repeated the words: "Bruce doesn't exist," hoping his mechanical mind worked the same way as a human's. Repetition turned short-term memory into long-term memory. Humans could only retain seven data points. They could be as simple as numbers or as complex as an entire sentence. The shorter the better as it reduced the chances of getting the order mixed up or confused in some way.

Everything began to grow dark. Felix finally realized why he was having second thoughts. He didn't want to die. It scared him. *I don't want to die. I don't want to … die.*

# 19

The interior of Kyle's ani-mech glistened with light. Unsure what was happening, he went with it and began to take the offensive. Azami jabbed and crossed shortly after. Kyle blocked the first with his hand and parried the other with his forearm. Before, he couldn't even defend himself. Now? He flipped around, grabbing Azami's ani-mech with his legs and performing a scissors takedown. The quieted audience erupted into celebratory cheer.

Still pinned down by his legs, Kyle trapped Azami in a choke hold and applied all the pressure he could, hoping she would tap out. She didn't and seemed to be getting stronger. It was probably all in his head, but Azami was definitely forcing herself free. Even during their training, she'd displayed an ungodly strength. The amount of effort she was putting into escaping was all her. No help from an AI like Yoshi.

Speaking of which, he was awfully quiet. Kyle found his grip loosening and his reserve power waning. He had a perfect grip on her ani-mech. She shouldn't be able to move, let alone this much.

"Yoshi, you there?"

No response. *The hell is he doing? I can barely keep her down.* It took all his muscles just to adjust his ani-mech's arms and legs, and he was barely doing that. Every second Azami came closer to releasing herself from his grip and winning the match. Kyle knew his advantage would be over as soon as he let go. No way she'd fall for the same trick twice. Of course, he wasn't sure why Yoshi decided to help him now and not earlier. The more he thought about it, the less sense it made.

"Stop thinking and focus on winning."

Kyle blinked. "Yoshi, is that you? What happened?"

Azami used this opportunity to escape. Once she did, her ani-mech stood there for longer than he expected. *Why doesn't she attack?* Could she be worried that the sudden surge of power wasn't a fluke and planning her next attack more carefully? He wished he knew what was going on inside her head.

Azami ran at him, full speed, her usual guard stance gone, replaced with pure offense. It seemed she planned on winning the battle with one final attack. But that wasn't her style. She always gauged an opponent's strength before going on the attack. Had she figured out his weakness in such a short time? And how come he wasn't aware of it? Also, it was getting harder to move. The hell was Yoshi doing with the strength percentages? Kyle scrolled through his HUD and noticed his reserve power was almost completely drained. *Ten percent? How the hell am I still able to move?*

It was an ani-mech AI's primary function to keep power eighty percent or above. Any less and at least twenty percent of the ani-mech's total mass was forced upon the fighter. Kyle knew he could move without an AI, but fighting and moving were different. Did something happen to Yoshi? With only ten percent of the ani-mech's weight not affecting him, his body should be crushed. Especially considering how badly she was knocking him around earlier. His body felt limp, and soon even his wrist became too heavy to move. He could barely squat without feeling the thousands of pounds of weight from the ani-mech applied to his muscles, which felt like jelly right now.

"I can't go on," Kyle muttered. "I give up!"

He activated the surrender protocol so his decision could be recorded as final and made public. Azami was better than him, than anyone else in a generation. He doubted even her father was this strong. Legends often distorted the reality of a person's accomplishments.

The crowd's silence from anticipation shifted to pent-up outrage at the result of the fight. He could see the headlines now. "Former Champion Surrenders: What it Means for the World." There'd be a bunch of op-ed pieces about how Azami would take the colony back to the dark ages of the twenty-first century. That a criminal shouldn't have been allowed to enter in the first place. Kyle scoffed at the imaginative thought. No doubt someone would accuse her of cheating. It may be a leap to believe everyone would hate Azami during her first term, but he wouldn't be around to see it. At least not in the light. Those same people who would hypothetically call Azami criminal couldn't say Kyle himself didn't fall in the same category. He killed Richard Piezo. Yes, it was allowed in the tournament, but that shouldn't matter. Murder was murder even if accidental. To say he wasn't a criminal when Azami was, reeked of lies people tell themselves to feel better. Hypocrisy at its finest.

The only thing worrying him now was his father's reaction. First thing's first, I need money. *If I can just slip out the back, then maybe I can beat the crowd to the bank.* Hopefully he could get there before his father froze all his assets.

## 20

BRUCE GRITTED his teeth and clenched his fist until his whole arm shook with uncontrollable rage. Everything he'd worked for, ruined by a seventeen-year-old—almost a decade of planning, gone. *There has to be a way inside that vault, but I've tried everything.* The will was clear. Azami needed to lose the tournament. Everything should've gone as planned. It was the ultimate chance to defeat her, and she somehow managed to overcome it. How!?

Even in death, his brother-in-law was one step ahead of him. Fei would pay for what he did to Bruce's sister. He could still remember seeing her helpless and barely clinging to life. What kind of man does something like that to his own wife? And to have his own daughter be the only one with the authority to do end it. Bruce took a deep breath and exhaled through his nose, creating a whistle as the air left his body.

Perhaps he was looking at this the wrong way. If Azami could see it, maybe she'd make the decision herself. He was out of options at this point and the potential risk was worth the reward. *God, what is wrong with me?* Talking about Yori like some sort of prize. No, what he wanted was to save her. A life like that was not a life at all. It had to be done.

Bruce dialed a number into the phone and placed the Redtooth earpiece into his right ear. The line rang for a few seconds before someone answered.

A woman spoke on the other end. "Yes, Mr. Strizynski?"

"She won."

The woman sneezed, and the sound of a chair rolling on hardwood filtered through the earpiece a second later. The audible motion was steady and unflinching, as if she'd expected this call.

"Very well, I'll go talk to her," Mrs. Cranston said. "I assume this means our business has concluded?"

"You tell me," Bruce said. "You're the one who started this."

"As far as my late client is concerned, it's over. Once the girl reads the will, it'll be up to her to do what she wants with it. It'll be out of your control."

## 21

Azami still couldn't believe it. Not that she won, but that Kyle put up a better fight than she'd anticipated. He'd come a long way in a few months. How did he manage to fight back at all? She thought it was impossible for Yoshi or Felix to fight her. Somehow, Kyle was able to overcome the protocol.

Speaking of Kyle, where was he? He couldn't be upset about losing, could he? They both knew she was going to win. It wasn't arrogance. He simply needed more training. In a year or two, he might be better than her. That would make the next tournament all the more exciting. Azami's more primal instincts made her giddy, but she stopped herself from squealing with delight. This was exactly what happened to her father. All the fame went to his head, and he wound up becoming an abusive husband and horrible father. Of course, to the outside world, Fei was practically a saint. His public persona was too evangelized, and when he committed suicide because of the divorce—forget it—nobody had believed her. They said she was too young to grasp concepts so dark and twisted. Yet by age ten she'd already known what it was like to lose everything.

Footsteps came her way, and Azami stood up, expecting Kyle. Instead, a woman in a business suit approached her. She had ebony dark hair and wore glasses with a reddish tint and sheen to the frame. When she reached Azami, she handed her a letter.

"This is for you. I represent your father and he wanted you to have this when the time was right."

Azami looked down at the letter and back at the woman. Upon closer inspection, she looked more like a porn star in an office scene where she played the secretary. God, was this one of his mistresses? She wanted to throw up. *Just when I thought I couldn't hate my father more, I find out he's a cheat.* Part of her wasn't all that surprised. A celebrity having sex with a porn star. Stop the presses.

"Let's pretend I understand a word of what you just said. Who are you?"

"I'm your father's lawyer, and I have his will here in this envelope. Everything should make sense after you've read it. Of course, if you don't, here's my card."

She handed her a business card. Azami put it away without looking at it. If the lawyer was telling her the truth, why come to her now? What kind of sick game was Bruce playing?

"How stupid does your client think I am?" Azami asked.

"My client is dead. I don't know what you're implying."

"Tell Mr. Strizynski that I'm not falling for it."

"Bruce Strizynski has nothing to do with why I'm here. As I've said, your father wanted you to have to this. My business with Mr. Strizynski concluded last year."

"Okay, which one is it then? Is the letter a will or something my father wanted to give me post-mortem? I dealt with this back when he died the first time. I burned them then and I'll do it again. So why don't you cut the crap and tell me the truth?"

"God, you're just like him," the lawyer said. "A total prick."

"What did you say?"

It was the second time someone called her father something negative. Even if she was lying about something, how could she possibly come to such a conclusion on her own? Unless she knew him. The real him. It was something only a member of the same household could know. Either that or someone who he could confide in. Azami doubted her father ever went to therapy. He certainly lied about it to the press after the divorce. It made his sob story all the more heart-breaking to the public eye when he killed himself. Perhaps this woman was his lawyer. But why come now?

Azami opened the letter and found directions inside the envelope. It wasn't to anywhere on the colony. In fact, she'd only been there once before. Back when she found out her father was still alive. "Alive" was loosely applicable here as he was just a machine. The masked fighter to everyone but those who knew the truth. Wherever her father wanted her to go—over a decade after his death—was on the Outskirts.

She looked up and the lawyer was already walking away. Azami reached into her pocket and pulled out the woman's business card. Deus Tech and its logo were nowhere to be found. If this was a ruse, they were certainly going all out.

Someone tapped her on the shoulder from behind, making her jump. It was Kyle. He said he needed to clean off, but he wore the same clothes as before. Someone needed to tell him about putting on clean clothes after a shower, she thought. He reeked.

"What's up?" Kyle asked. "You look distracted."

"It's … here just read this."

She handed him the letter, and his eyes went wide as he read it.

"This is from your father. An actual will. Didn't you already deal with this years ago?"

Azami nodded. "Look at the location. Whatever I'm supposed to inherit is on the Outskirts. Apparently, it's a vault of some kind."

"You seriously want to go back there?" Kyle said. "After what happened at the hospital? You don't need the money. Trust me."

"Of course not, but part of me is curious to see what he left me. Even if I won't know what to do with it."

Kyle sighed. "Well, I wish you luck, but I'm not going back there. We barely escaped the last time and I don't feel like dying quite yet."

"Suit yourself. Good luck with not being rich."

He smiled. "Are you kidding? This is the greatest thing that's ever happened to me. See you later. Next time you see me, I'll have made a name for myself."

~

THE CLIMATE on the Outskirts was much harsher this time of year. It didn't seem scientifically possible for the moon to change from a tundra to a desert in a matter of months, but Azami guessed that's what people back on Earth thought about the seasons way back when.

Azami wished she had left her coat at home. The clothing was meant for extreme cold conditions and tying it around her waist proved fruitless as it kept falling off. She didn't want to leave it as the temperature changed faster and more dramatically than the seasons.

"How much father is it?" Azami asked.

*I'm so exhausted I'm talking to myself.* And she'd just said "father" when she meant "farther." People might think she had the female equivalent of an Oedipus complex. So gross. What her mother saw in him, she'd never know. Nor did she want to understand.

Her interstellar GPS said a few more yards to go before she reached her destination. Only she couldn't see two feet in front of her with the sun's glare blinding her view the further east she went. Whatever was inside that vault better be worth it. The iGPS pinged, and the computer voice gave its arrival confirmation to her. All these technological breakthroughs, and yet we're still on "you have arrived at your destination." Azami shook her head, amused.

Whatever this place was, it made the former hospital look like a mansion by comparison. Why would anyone want this let alone keep it for their next of kin? It was smaller than her shop, minus the garage portion where she fixed ani-mechs. Even still, what the hell was so special that she needed to wait until now to see it? What purpose could her father have for keeping this a secret until she won a tournament? It was such an odd prerequisite. Did he honestly think she'd be daddy's little girl after everything he'd done? *Fat chance*, she scoffed and made her way around the side of the building, hand streaking across the unusually cold surface until she found an entrance.

She tried to open it, but the handle and door wouldn't budge. For a location to be so hot on the outside, it must be even colder inside the building. Either that or this place didn't obey natural weather laws. Azami rubbed her hands together to warm them up. She tried again, but the door still wouldn't open. First it told her to come here, now it won't even let her in? The hell kind of game was he playing?

"I knew this was a waste of time," she said in a huff.

"It's not," a familiar voice said.

*The hell is he doing here?* "I thought this moon was supposed to be dangerous. What are you doing here without your security detail?"

"Security implies I have the money to pay them," Bruce said. "I don't. Not anymore. I sold everything I had so you would lose the tournament. I was hoping to kill two birds with one stone, but alas ..."

"What do you mean 'two birds with one stone?'" Azami asked.

"It's an expression used to convey—"

"I know what it means, but you clearly wanted me to lose. That was the first bird. What was the second?"

Bruce smiled. "You always were a clever one, even as a little girl. My sister raised you well."

"Sister," Azami said, taking a step back and nearly falling backwards. "You don't mean . . . you're my uncle?"

"On your mother's side, yes. My real name is Bruce Tatsu, and I need your help to save your mother."

"My mother's dead. If you are who you say you are, you should already know that. Why'd you bring me here?"

"To tell you the truth, your father wanted to keep it secret. Your mother is alive, and she's in there."

Azami folded her arms. "How do you know?"

"Because that same letter was also sent to me. A last taunt from my brother-in-law. Like you, I thought my sister was dead. Until I received a letter from your father's lawyer, proving she was being kept in a cryogenic state."

"The police report," Azami said. "Your name was on it. As Bruce Strizynski. Why lie about your identity? If you told them you were her brother, they might have done something. They could've stopped it from getting worse."

"I did. I gave them dozens of chances to do the right thing and arrest him. After a couple months my reports weren't even making it past the secretary. So, I changed my name to give them another lead." Bruce sighed. "But by that point, the damage had been done. Your father committed suicide and locked your mother away here."

"You're wrong," Azami said. "I said goodbye."

"To an empty coffin. Surely, you must've thought it odd they cremated her before burying the body? Your young mind wanted to believe the world wasn't that bad. Eventually you realized the reality by yourself but never bothered looking into the truth of the matter."

Azami's mind darted back and forth from the past and present. She tried her best to remember the night her father killed himself, but it had happened so long ago, she couldn't be sure if what she remembered actually happened. *But why? Why would I want to forget my uncle? The one person left who could've taken care of me when I needed it the most.* The whole thing didn't make any sense.

"What aren't you telling me?" she asked.

Bruce raised his eyebrows and then smirked. It was the kind of smile a father gave to his daughter for doing something that made him proud. Azami waited so long to see that expression of happiness on someone else's face. She sniffled and wiped her nose, tears forming in both eyes.

"You look just like her," Bruce said. "The way your forehead wrinkles when something's bothering you. I think it'll be better if you see it for yourself."

He gestured to the locked door. Azami looked at him, confused. She already tried opening it. He must've seen her. Why did he want what was inside? And what exactly did he mean by looking just like her. If anything, she looked more like her father than her mother. Bruce reached for something next to Azami's face. Nothing was there and she felt uncomfortable having him so close. He smiled and pulled a quarter out from behind her ear. Azami was not amused.

Bruce sighed. "You used to love that. Guess I should consider myself lucky you believe me."

"Who said I believe you?"

"You're still here, aren't you?" He wiped off a thick layer of dust next to the door, revealing a virtual keyboard.

Azami folded her arms and looked away. He had a point, but the only reason she entertained the idea was because of her mother. Uncle or not, Bruce seemed to know and believe her about her dad. That was more than she could say for most people. At least now she knew how to enter and why Bruce couldn't gain access. Still, what was inside?

She entered the password Mrs. Cranston had given her. The lock mechanisms inside the latch creaked to life and the door opened— revealing machines and tubes—all connected to a single pod partly hidden in the shadows in the back of the room. It looked like a miniature spaceship. Azami found herself drawn to it and walked forward. Whatever was inside there, the man behind her wanted it badly enough to throw his own son under the proverbial bus.

She continued to walk toward the pod. The sound of Bruce's footsteps stopped a few paces back, but looking behind her, she saw him clear as day near the only way in or out. As she drew closer, tubes she hadn't seen before came into contact with her body. They were small, but not spider silk thin. She must not have noticed them due to focusing on the pod. A light fluctuated between blue and green like the calming glow of a hot tub at night. It made no sudden changes, keeping the same slow rhythmic pattern. Azami's hands began to tremble and sweat as she stood next to the pod. Her heart raced, and each breath became harder to enter or exit her lungs.

A sheet of fogged glass obscured the inside of the pod. She wiped the condensation from the translucent metal and jumped back the moment she saw what was inside.

"Who is this?" Azami asked. "Why does she have my mother's wedding ring around her neck? She'd never take that off. I can't … damn it, why did you bring me here?"

"Isn't it obvious? This is your mother, and I brought you here to kill her."

## 22

Azami's heart skipped a beat. *What did he say? Kill my mother? Why would I do something like that?* For so long she thought she was dead. To get a second chance to be with her, even in such a limited capacity, was almost too good to be true. In fact, she knew it was. This couldn't be her mother. The woman she knew didn't have blonde hair.

"The button's over there," Bruce said. "I trust you'll make the right decision. I'll be outside when you're ready. Take all the time you need."

Azami wiped her runny nose and sniffled. "She's your sister. How can you want her dead? We just found her and she's alive."

"That," he said, between heated exhales, "is not *living*! She's a slave in her body, just like when she was with Fei. Only now the body is her prison."

"But why kill her when she's still alive? That's murder."

"So is abortion. Hell, even suicide counts as murder according to society's laws. But you can't call that living. Not in any meaningful sense of the word. At the very least she's existing. But alive? No."

Bruce's argument made sense, but how could he want to kill her so soon after finding her? Unless ... he already knew where she was.

"How long?" Azami asked. "How long have you known?"

Bruce remained silent and looked away. His guilty gaze didn't last long and he turned his head toward her, eyes locked with her own. In a voice void of any doubt, he began to talk.

"I didn't know until after Fei's suicide. I received a letter from his lawyer," he continued. "She gave me this address and a photo with my sister where you see her now. In addition to the location, he left a message for me. The words: 'You'll never see her again' became etched into my mind. Eating and sleeping no longer came naturally as long as I knew she was still out there like some lab rat. So, I devised a plan to have you lose the tournament this year, and it failed. The registration updates, the masked fighter, Mr. Piezo, even my own son —they were no match for you. I see that now and am truly sorry. I should've been upfront with you from the start."

Azami's voice trailed off as she thought back to that night her father beat her mother to the brink of death. The image of her mother—bloody, broken, and beaten both in the mental and physical sense—made her furious. She felt a chill run down her back. Her mother had died then. She remembered the trauma vividly now. The memory she'd repressed for so many years now played back in slow motion inside her mind. It fractured her psyche to an almost irreparable state. She inhaled and exhaled repeatedly, panicking and afraid of every single noise. All the strength in the world didn't mean anything if she was too anxious to even breathe.

Ever since she was a girl, she hated Fei for being a bad father. Not once did she think about why he killed himself. For so long, she assumed her mother died after his suicide. Now that she knew the truth and all the painful memories it brought back, Azami saw her father's death not as a coward's way out but as a cry for help. One most people assumed didn't affect the rich and famous. Azami began reading the will in its entirety, including her father's suicide note photocopied and stapled to the back of the document. It said:

*What's the point in living if you're just invisible to everyone? Why bother continuing when you're only as good as what they think you're worth? My wife hates me and I can only imagine what my daughter thinks of me after seeing me at my absolute worst. It's been almost a year since I gave up alcohol and, if anything, my life is worse. I realize I've no one to blame but myself, but damn it people can change.*

Azami noticed a dried damp spot before the start of the next paragraph. It was like the man writing this note was a completely different person than the one who raised her. Where was this man when she and her mother were fearful for their lives? To show such compassion in words alone, to be able to both feel and see his feelings and thoughts like this was cathartic. She'd assumed for the longest time that she knew everything there was to know about her father. He was a monster and deserved no sympathy.

*Even an hour after her death, my hand still trembles. This one time I went too far and hurt the only person who ever cared for me. Even when I gave her no reason to show me any compassion. If anything, I owed her and now … I can't even do that. Maybe I am just a waste of space. It's certainly better than being seen as a monster by my own daughter. I might as well end it now. There's no coming back from this, and I at least want to die on my own terms.*

Azami's lip quivered as she placed a hand to her mouth and closed her eyes, holding back tears by gasping at air. Why was this letter so hard to read? It's not like she knew her father to be anything other than what he himself described in his note. Perhaps that was it. She didn't know her father on a level deeper than the surface. Here was a man who, according to most psychologists, should've been a dominating sociopath to everyone. Yet those who lacked empathy for others couldn't cry tears for people they loved. Regardless of how she felt about her father and mother's relationship, Azami knew that her father loved her.

"I'll be outside when you're done," Bruce said and left her to continue reading.

~

THE MOMENT BRUCE WENT OUTSIDE, the change in temperature made his sinuses act up. Going from cold to hot made his mucus liquify like jelly. The gelatinous substance inside his nose caused him to breathe through his mouth. Ten minutes passed without any sign of Azami.

Perhaps she didn't have the stomach for it. He couldn't really blame her, but he'd done all he could, and now it was up to Azami to make the decision. To be honest, it should've been hers from the start. He realized that now and felt worse than scum for trying to go around her and do the job himself. She may have been his sister, but Yori had married someone who, despite his alcoholism, loved his daughter enough to give her a choice when it was time to let go of the past.

Bruce smiled. He could learn something from his niece. She was only in her early twenties and already maturing into a fine young woman. *Despite our differences, you'd be proud of the woman she's become.* Strong like her father and stubborn like her mother.

The door opened, and his niece stepped out, her eyes red and puffy. Bruce looked at her in anticipation. Did she do it? The girl walked right past him and said nothing. She continued to remain silent for the remainder of the trip back to the station. He was about to ask what happened when a loud boom sounded behind them. Without turning around, he smiled and flew back home. Their pasts were both behind them where they belonged.

## ALSO BY MIKE BERGONZI

Moon and Star: Book One

Moon and Star: Book Two

Moon and Star: The Complete First Saga

# ACKNOWLEDGMENTS

This book would not have been possible, were it not for the Illinois Arts Council Agency. The IACA helped fund the majority of editing costs, formatting, and the initial marketing push. Special shoutout to my developmental and copy editors—Gillian Hill and Cody Sisco, respectively. Also thanks to fellow author Tim Niederriter for his work on the covers for the ebook and paperback editions.